You Don't Have to Say

Alan Beard

**Tindal
Street
Press**

First published in UK September 2010
by Tindal Street Press Ltd
217 The Custard Factory, Gibb Street,
Birmingham, B9 4AA
www.tindalstreet.co.uk

A CIP catalogue reference for this book is available
from the British Library

ISBN: 978 1 906994 12 9

Typeset by Alma Books Ltd
Printed and bound in Great Britain by
LPPS Ltd, Wellingborough, Northants

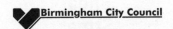

CONTENTS

To all my family, mum, dad and sisters
and Clare, Chloe and Grace

HOT LITTLE DANNY

After six months of signing on they send me to Josiah Mason College for 'work training'. Attendance compulsory: my benefits depend on it. The woman who takes General Studies wears a mid-length skirt-and-boots combination that my mother might have worn as a teenager in the seventies. She says her name is Mel – short for Melanie. 'Don't laugh, my parents were hippies.' No one is. She gets us to move our chairs into a circle to 'facilitate discussion'. I sit opposite her and think she looks all right for a woman her age. I like her sugary mouth, eyes that crinkle up easily, as if she is always amused. She tries to get us to talk about ourselves but we just grunt and look at the floor. So she talks instead about herself: she's thirty-nine, she mock cries about her forthcoming forties; she has no children – 'You are all the children I need!' – she laughs loudly to let us know she's joking. I'm watching her round knees and trying – probably all the boys are – to see more of her thighs as she moves on her chair.

*

'Go that way,' Jake is breathless. 'Get the fucker.'

'Where is the little runt?'

We are behind billboards on an arc of wasteland, rubble and brick and waist-high nettles down to the railway line. The runt, escaped from a pub car park, is hiding out there somewhere. We sweep out in a line, the four of us, like coppers on the news, searching the rough ground.

'There he is, there he is.'

He slips out of hiding, his white mesh cap not helping. Idiot, I think, enraged he could be so stupid.

Jake has him in a neck-lock. Mark holds his hands behind his back. The kid's face is red with denial. He didn't do it. Jake rips open his shirt, with difficulty. The runt twitches his nose at me.

'Burn him, Danny, burn him.'

The cigarette between my fingers I use as a pen, put a big full stop on his tit, above the nipple. A train goes by behind him as I do it.

'Teach you,' I say.

*

We go back to Jake's, a place he's buying from our joint proceeds. Dirt cheap anyway on the estate of red-brick sixties housing and brown tower blocks. The electric chugs as wires crumble in the walls, lights flicker, the music wavers. Mice run along the skirting.

Cheers, I say to Mark who says I did well out there, and feel good because I'm one of the youngest in this late-teen project. Him and Jake in their mid-twenties are the oldest, direct things, deal with banks and building societies.

On my way upstairs I pass a topless girl sat smoking, leant forward so her tits rest on her knees, one arm crooked around them; pink peeks out.

They joke in the kitchen about my age, friendly cuffs and smiles from teeth already brown, cutting up dope and listening to one of the radios tuned to the police frequency.

'Schoolboy Danny! You're too young to smoke.'

'Nah,' I say, 'I left months ago.'

When the pill kicks in I go back to the girl on the stairs to taste her smoky breath and feel her hands on me. She is soft and white, orange freckles across her shoulders, a mouth that opens slowly.

Nothing rasps: for a while we flow somehow, like things melted together. After, I pull myself up to a sharpness and join in the backslapping and high fives below the stairs I leave her on. Mark and Jake talk about next operations, mainly drug deals and distribution, but also a warehouse robbery. My part in it they discuss like I'm not there – delivery, collection, and, after tonight, enforcement.

I move about the house leaving a swathe of colour, laugh at two snorting Shazzes on the sofa making a mess over their touching knees; go outside to see the night set deeply, the estate settling to sleep as we begin. Then I jump back into the music and thrash about like something caught and pulled out of water, gleaming, catching the light as I twist about.

*

Days without drugs are like drinking pond water, each minute a piece of weedy scum. Even the birds sound strangled in the trees. People are too present, their fingernails and hair, their squinting looks, their dirty skins. My joints ache, my eyes begin to jelly up. I go back to Mum in Selly Oak.

As I reach the door Jerry Hughes walks past, my best friend when I was nine, ten, eleven years old. Sat next to him one year in primary school; stuck sticks down drains with him. I remember playing hide-

and-seek in the car park at one end of our street, crouched, cheek against the concrete to look under the vehicles for a glimpse of his ragged trainers. His dad when he was alive had a booming voice which you could hear even if you were at the wrong end of the street, near the three-lane Main Road, bristling cars. 'Hi Jerry,' I say but he scuttles past, dragging his bad leg, scared, which makes me smile.

Mum hears the key in the lock and comes down the corridor swishing her skirt; thinking aloud about her sister, Aunt Julie, who is having a mastectomy today she tells me.

'Julie, Julie you're all right. Say it with me, Danny: Julie, Julie you're all right.'

She's as insomniac as me, not taking her medication, making me four-sugared coffees and gabbling about when she was a girl, friends and enemies who imprisoned her in a hedge, or made fun of the twitch she used to have.

The air smells faintly of farts. I stay to catch up with all the family news. It takes a few days now to get it all from her distracted thoughts, distracted for ever by my long-gone father. He was always disappearing for days, and finally went for good. I would watch his white car with the yellow sticker advertising an arts cinema on the side window, wait with the winker going, to turn into the traffic.

Occasionally we'll go visiting, take buses to Yardley and Erdington. I play the dutiful son while I climb down carefully from some place in the sky. I sit around with aunts and uncles and cousins and friends, invariably in the kitchen sipping tea. I've watched the new additions to the family grow from crawl to stumble to walk, seen them fight over toys, and heard them learn to swear. The older ones live perpetually twenty years ago, trying to recreate their before-you-were-born world, lighting fags and fetching photo albums and vinyl albums in cardboard covers coming apart.

Then I have to get with my mates. Do stuff. Smudge everything with drugs, weed at least. Go out and bloody the night with flame. Set an old building alight, stand around in its glow until the cops come. We will get to it along the canal, holding cans of petrol, kicking out at the geese we disturb, darkness coming down and moths around like rags of mouldy cotton.

I walk through Selly Oak on my way to the Castle. I walk past the massage parlours – Emmanuelle's, the Hideaway Club, Manyana – the empty shops covered in fly posters, the cafés and takeaways. I dodge through groups of students in fur-lined coats, the girls with koala bear bags, the blokes with little Vs of beard and sideburn, on their way to and from the university. Or who stop, slowly counting out change among fruit stands outside Asian mini-marts, arranging to meet in the Varsity.

*

Some hymn or pop song – *for ever, for ever more* – I'd heard somewhere set the mood as I went into town with my crowd. Down Broad Street, a CCTV celebrity, I led, an arrow that cut through the glad-ragged hordes and glanced off pub and club doors as we were refused entry. Light and drink and girls within, music pouring out, smells of perfume, smoke and beer to go with the flashing legs around. The families on their way through to the cinema wary of the likes of me, leering into their faces, singing and waltzing with the wife if I get a chance, little pirouette and bow for them at the end.

She said she'd seen me dancing in one of those bars that let us in, the Sports Bar maybe or Revolution, stopped me from going out of class to tell me, and asked to take me for a meal – out of town, she added quickly – as if it was something she asked all her students.

She drove down to Worcestershire, a town by the wide river. A vegetarian restaurant, green paintwork. A cannibal wouldn't have been more out of place. She wore jeans and fake gold jewellery and her made-up eyes looked around, her head held back a little as if she was sniffing the air. She pointed out the colour of the salads in their bowls, red bean, rice, a tray of quiche. On the wall a poster of a man in a gas mask, above him 'No Smoking', below 'People are Breathing'.

Waiting for her to pay the bill I rolled a fat one, leaving shreds of tobacco and dope over the table and lit it on the way out.

*

The man we stop to rob on early-hours streets has large swollen cheeks and chin, all stubble, a wave of black hair on his forehead, dyed must have been, a dead cigarette, creased blue shirt, creased grey trousers, cracked trainers.

'All right lads?' He asks with drink on his breath. 'Want a fag or something?'

We follow him, turn a corner behind him. I know we won't get much out of him but instead of leaving it I take it out on him as he blubbers from his hit mouth, because he's there, in the wrong place, where there should have been someone richer.

*

Greeny-yellow smear across the rain-windows of trains. The blurt of city. Coming out of stations, I glimpse Shazzes pushing babies along; unwarming coats flap. Snow then, like wet paper around, it doesn't fall, it doesn't appear to fall, it just fills up the air.

The criss-cross I make across the city on my missions, alighting in odd places I've never been before, watching out for local lads. But I'm OK, I don't stand out when I don't want to; none of the baseball cap, the Burberry, no tattoo on the neck, no piercings, just me slipping past you in the night.

Most are easy, give in, promise to pay, do pay. I'm not that big so I get the easier ones, carefully chosen. Schoolkid; skinny; the just-at-work with spare money. The scared already.

I watch a family emerge from the swimming pool, come out of the lit building into the dark. The little girl with wet hair plastered to her cheeks, in red skirt and white socks, skips with delight into the car park. The boy who owes us wears an anorak and jeans, and bashes his frizzed head with a rolled towel.

'Oy!' I urge from the side. I don't care about grown ups, fathers, usually as piss-scared as their offspring. Besides, in my coat pocket, my fingers already curled around the handle, I have a hammer. Jake says guns will – might – come later.

She talks on the bed about *I'm a Celebrity* – eating bugs.

'I'd do it,' I say. 'Dip my hand in to get bit or stroked.'

She laughs, strokes.

'They'll have public floggings next. You probably, when you're caught, in Centenary Square where the old statue was, and filmed live by *Midlands Today*.'

'Central,' I say.

'Central,' she corrects herself.

She likes to come around my house when Mum is out, once a week or so in the daytimes, 10-2, she puts it down as travelling time, being peripatetic. She is amazed to come to this three-storey near the university, had expected a tower block flat maybe. She likes the view across the red buildings of the uni – she went there – to the Italianate tower. She likes my 'spermy boudoir' in the attic, the *Kerrang* posters, put up when I was eleven, just after Dad left, corners hanging off the sloping roofs. She likes my unwashed toes, my vigorous swearing, my soft stubble, my body – not muscly, but strong, she says.

She gets giggly sometimes on the dope we smoke before and after lying on the creased bed or pretending to listen earnestly to music she's brought around. She is retro, pop music sustains her. She's into people I've never heard of. Syd Barrett – the same four songs, 'the rest are crap' – taped over and over again on a 90-minute tape, because she 'wasn't up to speed' with CD burning. 'Wined and Dined', 'Dominoes', she repeats the titles as they play over and over into my room that has heard nothing but rock when I bothered to play anything.

She talks of her childhood in a village somewhere outside the Lake District with woods and a stream that was gradually spoiled by a slag heap built nearby. The neat little patch of houses, some half-timbered, the giant pub, smaller church and bridge. She sounds like Mum now, but I don't tell her so. Got surrounded by landfills and rubbish tips, she says, shaking her head, a whole new hill built up behind her house as she grew. A smell always there, worse in summer, plagues of flies, seagulls coming inland, lorries rumbling up and down the narrow roads. So she came to the city and liked the comforts: buses, trains, cinemas, pubs, the density of people warming you through. And variety. A variety of men. Her husband one of them? I ask, and she shushes me, doesn't want mention of him, never does. I don't know what he does or how old he is or if he's any good in bed.

I tell her of when I was eight in the Chinese takeaway. The telly in the top corner, two women from the massage parlour dressed in short white 'doctor's' coats watching it. The one at the formica counter with the long, loose-curled perm, black against her white shoulder, makes to clip Chie's ear, same age as me but not in school much. She steps back to light a fag and points at me. 'Serve the young gentleman.' But then she looks over me at Dad coming in. 'Watcha, Deek.' She blows a lipstick kiss at him. I'm looking at the pink between the buttons of her coat. So is Dad.

Mel says I'm articulate and observant. She says if I was in her class I'd get triple As. She says to call her Miss and to tweak her rubbery nipples like the naughty boy she knows I am.

*

Mum said she'd forgotten how to enjoy herself. I persuade her to sit and chat with beer, I nearly roll a spliff.

'My eyes are always sore,' she said. 'Like they were then, when he was here, when he'd sit down and have a "reasonable" talk with me. Take his voice out for a long walk. He'd speak soft, slow as if to a dimwit. Each affair he confessed to with regret, as if he was forced to act that way. My eyes would start going then, blinking first, I'd fight that and then feel them go cold as I kept the lashes apart. His voice seemed to enter me there, through the pupils.'

*

I get to go to Mel's when her husband's away for a week. Shame to let the opportunity pass she says, but looks out for the neighbours when letting me in. She wears stockings all week. She keeps apologizing for non-existent cellulite.

On shelves, leaning against books, are photos of him now with grey receding hair ('older than me,' she explains, deciding she can't any more ignore his existence), his close-together eyes that seem grey too, and the tight smile, and then ('well before I knew him') graduating with long hair curling down from his mortar board. I say university people are slippery and mean or too locked up in their own worlds – the arts side at least. She laughs. My dad's a film lecturer, I say, I should know.

I pad around in my boxers like the man of the house, looking at all the rooms: posters, plants, cushions, shelves of books, an exact opposite to the bareness, apart from technical equipment, of Jake's. She comes out of nowhere to pat my arse.

'Get back to bed, you.' She buries the tied condom deep in the rubbish in the bin.

Lying next to her with her knees up, the view along her thigh, the sheen, the curve, we talk more. I tell her of being sat out the back with Jerry Hughes from up the road, feeling weary of him acting like a horse or something, on all fours. I hear Mum's chopped-up voice through the kitchen window, talking to silent Aunt Julie. 'It's the woman in him they love' . . . 'preening' . . . 'stays away like a cat'.

'Following in his footsteps?' says Miss Teachy-pants. She opens her legs more to let my fingers in. 'What else?'

At first when he'd really gone, Mum would take me over to his place, drop me off, and his new Shaz, someone from his faculty, hair done up like she's expecting the Queen, would serve up an evening meal, too much for a child, and I could sense the woman's fear when she turned to me. First time I'd seen it – the tensed shoulders, her bosom on show in a low-cut blushing. The sidelong approach, as if looking for escape: fear of me, an eleven-year-old. Dad wasn't interested in how we reacted, talked films to us both as if Steve Buscemi was one of his best pals.

'Cool,' says Miss Muckylips.

She liked the pictures she says, as a youngster she dreamt of an afternoon that never ended, of going into the cinema to see the best movie ever made and you are so comfortable and the movie so beautiful it can never end and you never come out to the pavement again.

I like to remember this when I see her amongst us young unemployed getting down with it, using Eminem phrases, and moving her hands, fingers stretched and bent like an American rapper as she talks about filling in forms properly, and how not to approach an interview. No one ever reacts, especially not me watching her prissy-looking mouth, the pink gums and straight teeth, full of advice and education, knowing soon it would be full of me.

*

I have to really hurt someone. Cut him. Drown him, threaten to, and really do it if he doesn't begin payment, plus beg for an hour or two. I follow him from his estate home on the bus to his stinky job where he wears a tie. Think of it as taxes, I'm going to say.

I've seen myself drown him so many times, or else sliding him, already dead, into the canal for the geese to honk over. I've seen his face bloated, distorted by the water so many times that when I see him on the street at the bus stop with the other geek clerks, the newly-at-work, singing in their clerk hearts that the day has ended, his perky face doesn't look right, the drug-snuffling pretty nostrils he has totally wrong; his tight mouth should be out of shape, grinning within water-stretched cheeks.

But when it comes to it I can't do it. Can't push the knife in, cut the bugger a bit. Followed him back on the bus, he looked back as he got off, and turned him round by the steps to his building. The door to the block opens with a noise like a kid's shout. In front of me the man is trying to stand straight in his sticky tie and poor checked shirt. I can't make the final thrust. Should do, quickly, and turn and disappear. No CCTV here but even if there were, they'd just see me brush past, maybe he wouldn't even fall straight away. But though I will it, it doesn't happen.

*

I told her Dad taught me to respect the main road – the only thing I remember him teaching me – after Jerry Hughes had been run over in front of my eyes, not killed but broken up for weeks. And how my mum made me go round his house, even though I'd dropped him after falling in with older lads who said he was a geek. Mum gave me a present to take round, a puzzle we could play together but we didn't, though I autographed his cast with a green felt-tip kept nearby for the purpose. He lay on the sofa smelling like stale biscuits, pyjama leg cut to accommodate the off-white plaster. His mother, Dottie, made me watch a video of when she and her husband won a prize on *The Price is Right*. 'It was a bathroom suite,' she said, 'the one you used today.'

Mel told me of her Selly Oak days – there before I was – or maybe I was just born, pushed in my chair by Mum across the road to Sainsbury's. I might have seen her pass, her student arse in combats or whatever they wore in those 'Thatcherite' days on my baby eye level. Dungarees or ra-ra skirts, she said, depending. She spoke of the political involvement then, marches and petitions, plans to bring down governments, but also the 'discos', being chatted up among the deep library shelves, sex in the halls of residence. She switched then to talk like a teacher about 'safely navigating' my adolescence, about being careful. I watched her eyes flicker over me, as if storing me up in her memory.

*

At Jake's the mice pepper everything we eat. A coming-down, early-hours pastime is hunting out their nests, killing them with sticks, always saying we will fry them and eat them with chips but we never do.

Not any more. I didn't do as told.

Jake explained things to me. Didn't I realize we were a feeder group, a branch allowed to operate at a low level, watched for talent, monitored for trouble? I hadn't been there long enough, obviously, and now never would be.

'Well,' he said pinching my arm in a grip that hurt, 'it's good we find things out in time.' He lifted his hand at any possible explanation. 'It's OK. No big deal. You just drop out, no spoils of war. You can still score here if you want, come to a couple of parties. We won't be here long anyway.'

*

When I see her in the Broad Street pub, sat with colleagues from work or somewhere, and see her arm around not her husband but some bearded twat, thirty-something and probably 'into' his career, I see her look across and catch my eye and the slight 'no' shake of her newly tousled hair. She turns back, pitching strongly into the conversation around her, shouted above the music, across the line up of half-full pints and bottles of Bud and cocktail glasses, not looking back.

I'll fly above the crush of people to her, to make a nuisance of myself, be her bad pupil. I'm on my way across when there's about five emerge from the crowd, one of them is the runt, marshalling his own mini-gang. Arms coming out to grab me from the crush of drinkers, bodies up against me, knees push at the back of my legs, a feel of steel through my shirt.

I hear snatches as they push, words as they edge me out of the pub.

'Burn him.'

'Peel him.'

'Kill him.'

I try and tear my eyes through to her corner across and through the muzzy crowd to where she is absorbed in her mates and her news and her future. I'm bundled and prodded, knifed lightly in the shoulder. The blood drops from me as I'm out in the street a while, rolling within the crowd, the near-naked Shazzes thinking I'm drunk, down a side street by O'Neill's, a few more cuffs and kicks and stabs out of CCTV range and I'm left with the blood and snot hanging from my nose and mouth, head down, my balls sore, feeling ruptured, leaking.

Wouldn't she like me like this, couldn't she tend to my wounds in her house above the city?

My head down to let myself leak I see first his

cracked trainers, then his creased grey trousers, his wave of dyed black hair.

'Got a fag?' he asks, leering out of the night, the crowd going by behind him, wrapping his arms around me, and legs, whispering, ooh, OK now, OK now, as we fall, entwined, to the ground.

*

I remember waiting at the pelican crossing on the main road thinking of Jerry Hughes and his flight into the air. How he landed near me and spots of his blood appeared on my jeans and trainers. I notice a pall of smoke move up, darker than the sky, and suddenly the roof of the massage parlour is in flames, tiles cracking and sliding off. The white car with the yellow sticker draws up, middle lane, three cars back, Dad inside on his way back. He winds down his window to see better the leap of flame and smoke like blood pumping up. Tiles smash on the pavement in bursts of shrapnel. Mum is out, she'll return to find him cooking, making amends. Between them, sometimes, I saw bouts of love that lasted months.

BACKING UP

The weekend, another day away, can't come quickly enough. I've had it. I was late this morning anyway because the old lady who stands by her door and asks passers-by what day it is called me over. It's Thursday, I said but she asked me to get her some Wilson's Menthol, pressing money into my hand. So I retrieved a tin from the corner shop that keeps a supply in just for her, apparently, and she tells me the history of her snuff habit. Her son complained about it, she said, going on and on in the corner till he left. The girls she worked with after the war (in a sandpit as far as I can make out) all did it. Her name's Mrs Churchill, like the prime minister, not that insurance dog. She stood in the cold in her slippers, a little blood in one nostril, blue eyes strong amidst the broken capillaries, and invited me in, not for the first time, to see the shrine to her dead husband in her front room, but I explained I had to go. Buses to catch.

Then the computer doesn't boot up properly when I get in and I have to defragment the hard disc, and back up files just in case. I can't get to my email or calendar so go to see John to see if he knows what's going on today. I know there's something on. I turn the corner to find him with George, who used to work here.

'I was brought up on white bread and fish fingers –'

'. . . finest breaded cod,' says George, who's now in Hepatology.

'. . . from a shop that was a greengrocer, a chemist –'

'. . . and a sub post office.'

Then another bloke with Jasminder comes out of the lift at the end. Ching.

'Two-one, two-one,' both of them burst out at George.

'That was weeks ago.'

'Cuppa, George?' John asks. 'Apparently there's a salesman somewhere,' he says to me. 'Go find him, Steve. It's your job to meet and greet.'

'Is it fuck.' My head drumming.

Too much too early in the week has done it. A Greek meal, someone's birthday, someone Val works with – she's trying to impress at the moment – so we had to go. I felt awkward over the feta cheese and retsina, council policies discussed, in-jokes about someone not there, but afterwards we parted into groups, and our bunch turned out to be lively. We ended up with more drinking and drugs in some half-empty club in the centre, half-heartedly lit in red and blue. I met Pete there, hadn't seen him in ages.

As I leave to find my salesman Jasminder comes after me, her light scent slightly before her.

'Here's the plan tonight: we get wrecked.'

'And then it's: don't you threaten me with a dead fish,' adds her companion, behind her.

'You going to introduce us?'

'Nah, he's . . . another Steve, I think, aren't you? Over for the presentation. Fellow Bluenose, recognized him from matches.'

'The presentation!' I slap my head to get it working but instead send waves of pain through it. Giddily, I go look for the salesman.

So the following night, last night, I went round Pete's, after a night drinking in Utopia, smoking dope in his murky flat, filling the room with exhaled smoke and reminiscences of old girlfriends and pubs we have known. I get up to look at the view of the blue/silver protuberance of Selfridges.

'Is Val the one then?' he asks as I've been with her for eight months now.

'Got any more lager?'

*

I tell the salesman about the presentation, how I'd forgotten and it's a three-line whip and so better if he came back. His equipment will help, he says, projectors you can link to computers, Windows compatible. He's got brochures on interactive whiteboards. Can't he stay and see? Even through the fug of headache I hear a grey pleading in his voice. In my head I'm listing our shared interests: drink, of course, she doesn't mind those green bottles lining up along the side of a room, on the side of the bath. We both like old Hollywood films and Sundays we get stoned and watch battle-of-the-sexes comedies, or shout along with James Dean in his arguments with his father. We both especially like films from the fifties – the hairdos, the monsters, the milkshakes – though neither of us knows why, except maybe it's our parents' youth we like to see.

'I'll ask.' I go back to see John to see if this is OK. He's more interested in telling me about his nine-year-old who fell out of a tree last night and scraped her face. There's a red scar across her eye, cheek to forehead. He demonstrates with his hand across his face. He's come late to kids, he says, so appreciates them more, but worries he hasn't got the backbone for it.

'It's all lifting and swinging around.'

He notices me wince and raises his gone-grey eyebrows like a headmaster.

'Rough night?'

'Ugh,' I nod. He reminds me of the presentation, and I remember the salesman.

'I can't put up with sales talk today. I've even forgotten what he's selling. Can I just send him away?' I'm no longer feeling charitable.

'OK.'

I turn to leave and Jasminder rushes in. It feels like I'm in a radio play. I expect banter, football talk. They always exchange Blues gossip, rumours of transfers, the delights of Dugarry, but she says there's someone on the roof. Threatening to jump. She says it in two sentences. Again I think – a joke, it's all jokes and japes this end of the corridor. But it isn't.

*

We work in a separate block in the hospital grounds, don't see many actual patients, except on your way in and out. First past A&E where a collective fuzziness comes off the drugged and damaged patients waiting there. (Some are still there, I'm sure of it, on the way back eight hours later.) Along the corridor where a dull silver lift opens to eject a bed pushed by nurses, an old woman with wispy hair turning the sharpest of faces at you. Worse are the bald or bowed younger ones who look away. Past the alcoves of vending machines and toilets, the painted floor stripes promising to take you to Renal or Cardiovascular. Make way for doctors responding to bleepers, running with ties flying, briefcases half open. Jasminder reckons they do it for effect.

We're through the back exit, away from the main part, green three sides of us. Over the last few days I've seen the Trust's gardeners, sat on tilting machines, give the slopes their last mow this autumn. Behind us a line of trees, a strip of yellow, red and brown now, leaves shedding in the breeze.

There's a car park at the front where the zigzag fire escape lands. It goes up to the flat roof – the man must have climbed it, passing the top-floor Medical Library and scaring Donna perhaps stood photocopying her sixth article from the *BMJ* and *Heart and Lung* to fax across to Doctor Bisnauth, even though they're available on the net. I work at the other end of the corridor, near the toilets, nothing but a clerk but you need a degree to do it, filing results emailed from across the campus and the regional hospitals' network. My job is to transform them into graphs, understandable presentations: PowerPoint, Camtasia. Some analysis then, brainwork, charting the spread of a disease or its demise, but not much. On the bus here this morning I wondered how Mrs Churchill would figure in a chart, and about Wilson's Menthol keeping its factory open just for her.

*

The boss comes up just as I'm saying goodbye to the disappointed salesman, to say no one is to leave. In case he jumps on top of us, I suppose.

We move around awkwardly, suddenly wanting to go across to the main building for newspapers and to consult colleagues, until finally we linger close to the window, seeing people gather in the car park below. I see Marsha, the nurse from A&E, a mole the shape of a blobbier Scotland on her temple; the cooks are there, the chief one like Shrek, except with more hair. Scare the bloke to jump, says Jasminder, coming up. Across the way is the eight-storey hospital, like our building made from sixties slab concrete, rain-stained and as cold as sky. I can see patients' faces line up along the bottom of the high-up windows.

The fire brigade arrives. Father Gillespie, the hospital priest, used to hearing last words, comes over from the elderly acute ward, red in the face from running across. He has his communion kit in its special suitcase with him. Emergency bread and wine. He calls up – Does he want anything? Had he something he wanted to say?

'Want Chrissie.'

I get close enough to hear his answer and see his legs dangling over the edge above, the soles of his trainers have an elaborate pattern like a tyre, stripe of Villa-colours sock and strip of flesh showing. Just above the top of the window. I see his hand come down by his knee, the thumb rotating the wheel on one of those throwaway lighters; a little flame keeps going out there.

'Go get Chrissie.'

We speculate on his age from that high-pitched voice struggling with four syllables, and decide no older than me – twenty-five. Probably younger. We take it in turns to crouch below the sill and look up to see more of him, except John who says his back won't take the crouching.

There's a silence that Jasminder breaks with a joke about other Villa fans joining him, notably our boss, who rang up from downstairs to ask people to stay away from the windows.

Then the man's legs go up as if a puppeteer has pulled strings. He's going across the roof, taking some of the crowd with him, who will stand on the slopes of wet grass making them muddy, red leaves swirling at their feet. I wonder if someone from the abundance of helping professionals on site isn't now climbing the stairs on the other side, ready to dash across to save/capture/arrest him.

*

We stand in doorways holding pieces of paper to show we are working, and exchange the latest information. Someone hears a radio report on WM and says Dave Dodd, who the man is, had an argument with his girlfriend about money and hit one of his step-kids, running off when she called the cops.

I notice the salesman unfold his laptop, and sit it on his knees. I rumble with aches. I think about phoning Val but her job's more important than mine, the kind of job where they meet to plan to have planning meetings. Besides, what would I say? We're surrounded by police and priest and hospital workers, outpatients on their way home from various clinics, medicine in pockets, waiting for a body to fall?

People get out lunch, I scrounge a banana for the salesman who seems to have become my responsibility but he refuses, crunching his way through Maltesers he must have brought with him. I sit next to him. Instead of commenting on

Roofman he goes on about the projector he's still willing to demonstrate if I can find a suitable room. He takes out a tissue and blows hard, tucks the article away quickly.

'Are you all right, Stan?' He's told me his name.

'Got three months and I'll tell you.' There is saliva running in his voice, mashed chocolate.

'Be with you in a minute,' I say and drift to the corner, then round out of sight to my office.

The computer seems to be functioning properly now, and for the next hour or so I do some work, after replying to emails. Medical Photography has emailed pictures of operations to me to caption. 'This is crap stitching by Mister Blunderhands, nothing new there' I put on one where you can see the bone showing through a shoddy flap of skin over a smashed knee. I delete and put 'X-pattern stitching . . .' The next batch in the mail is a man with stumps for fingers in physio.

I letter, cut and paste, jig the images about for maximum illustrative impact, remembering doing something similar with scanned-in shots of Val, only a few so far, eight months' worth. I want pictures of her past, her childhood, her student days but haven't been able to ask her yet, in case she thinks I'm weird. I want pictures from her future. I start singing, in the depths of my ragged brain, a cheesy disco song.

I check my eBay sales – I'm flogging dance music, can't be bothered with it much any more. Then again, I can't get into the recycled rock music that's around now. Finish off with some acetates wanted for the computerphobes on the Renal Ward. I print out pictures of the dialysis machine: its buttons, and instructions, a patient attached to it. I stick them in the internal post tray, then I have to go for a piss.

I meet Jasminder on my way out the door.

'Working? In all this excitement?'

'Umm.'

'Would you ever?' she says, leaning back. I see how leggy she is in those black tailored trousers, note again the cheekbones and nose I never stop noticing. She's told me about the arranged marriage she's about to enter into. I'm cool about it, she said, and showed me a photograph of her intended, from India – Pardeep, she said, as if she'd often repeated the name to herself.

'Would I ever what?'

'Jump. Commit suicide. Say, for love?'

'Don't be daft,' I chortle, making a deliberate noise in my throat as I try to watch her without showing it too much. Her dark absorbing eyes, the lightness of movement as she stands upright from the radiator. I move off, shaking my still-aching head to put Val back in there and see her again dancing with her mates, full of *keftedes* and

Bacardi Breezers, dancing to old skool stuff. When I got up to join them, I now remember, she said I was not my usual sharp self, wrapping her arms around me to keep me upright.

'Have you heard? He's leaving Friday,' Jasminder calls after me.

'Who?'

'Robinson Crusoe.'

*

While I piss, coffee turning the arc off-yellow, almost green, I think of the curve from Val's hip to her navel where I laid my cheek the other night, the smoothness against my bristle. I get a semi thinking of seeing her tomorrow night, Friday. I have everything ready: the sofa, the wine, the dope, the Sade album – our ironic homage to all things romantic.

I sing 'Smooth Operator' to the mirror: my fillings show blue.

I forget about Villasocks until I hear him shouting, a sound delivered by hidden duct to the toilet. A higher pitch than it could really have been. Its shrillness aggravates my hangover as if I'm being force-fed ice-cream.

'For fuck's sake jump, you cretin,' I say aloud and then worry the same duct will pipe my voice directly back to his ear so stealthily he'll think it's inside his head.

As I leave, zipping up, I look up to see fat trainers descending, out of the ceiling, jeans coming through, a growing beer belly under a maroon football shirt. Then his face with stiff whiskers, lumpy spots and shaved head bobs between the upstretched arms that drop him now from the skylight. Leaves come down with him, a roll of cold air taking them past me along the linoleum.

'You want me to jump?' He had heard. His eyes are screwed tight to focus on me in the dark corridor. He starts moving his hands as if practising for imminent assault. Instead of shouting, ducking, running I stay still. My headache, my tiredness, emptiness holds me there, or maybe the force of his stare.

'Chrissie was all right till she came here.'

'She's not here though.' I am within throttling distance but I must look defiant, brave, stupid or something, rather than just transfixed I think, my head involuntarily playing over and over Val's face as she bends to kiss me, the curve of her mouth like Lee Remick's in *The Europeans*, because he wavers.

'She'll be watching on local TV.'

He then gets so close I can count the crop of spots on one side of his mouth. The cold of his hours on the roof can't hide the smell of sweat, or maybe it's something else, I don't know, twenty years of tinned food, ten of chain-smoking. Like me, then. His arms go round me, a hug. I can feel his cock pressed up near mine. I try to manoeuvre out of this clinch. He says, 'D'you find it hard to breathe sometimes?' His breath and slobber on my cheek. I think of all the things I know about her – the strawberry key fob she has among the sliding things in her bag, the hard grey callous on one little toe, the deliberate walk – a parody of sexy – she puts on when she sees me.

'You OK?' Steve 2 shouts out, coming down the corridor, but I notice he doesn't leap to get him off. Dave Dodd, Villasocks, Roofman, breaks off of his own accord. He doesn't collapse or fight or howl, but turns, goes slowly to the window/fire exit at the end of the corridor. We two Steves watch him go, see Donna scuttle back into the library office out of his way. We both wonder, I know, if we should stop him, hang on to him while we get help, but we don't, we watch him clamber through the window and go up the stairs outside and on to the roof. I think I hear cheering.

We go to check if Donna's OK, and she is, just indignant that her routine has been broken into; she goes off to work in the library leaving us in her office. We speculate on Roofman's girlfriend and kids, and whether he'll jump or not; we both think not. Then we talk about other weirdos – er, vulnerable people – we have known, and agree that Jasminder is a real babe. Not only that, my namesake says, but she's a true Blue, born within hearing distance of the St Andrew's crowd, and taken by her brother to games when there were still terraces. I'm impressed but wonder if she'll still go when her husband arrives. Maybe she'll take him along. I tell him about Mrs Churchill's shrine to her husband. Containing, she'd told me, lined up on top of the dresser, his old umbrella, a 'special silver' pen he never wrote with but liked to click its nib in and out and kept in the top pocket of his storeman's overall, the cup he used all the time, and a picture of him receiving his long-service watch from the factory, now closed down. Though I'd never met him he seemed more familiar to me than my dad.

I invite Steve out with Pete and me next week and say maybe I'll join them tonight, depending on my head, still throbbing. We're back discussing Jasminder – she's mine, I saw her first – when she walks in, and try changing the topic to Donna's Medline searches, the printouts lined up alphabetically on the desk. Then we remember Villasocks and recount our brave attempts to keep him talking until help could arrive. My new-found mate backs up my lies. Jasminder confirms that local TV is actually here.

'Bad,' she adds. 'He'll be up there ages now. He'll want drink, food, fags brought up.'

'Like *Dog Day Afternoon*.' I say. 'Attica, Attica.'

'Don't think he's much like Al Pacino though.'

'I can vouch for that.'

George appears at the door and squeezes into Donna's narrow office. '*There* you are.' And we Steves tell again of Dave Dodd and my grapplings with him, how I had him round the neck. George says he's angry, shouting about his partner shacking up with another guy. John, following after him within a minute, peeling an orange, the zest flavouring the air, says he's pining for love, for his step-kids. He passes a segment through the crowd to me – 'Vitamin C, Steve.'

Donna is now in the doorway, returned from the library with bound journals in her hands, her head bobbing between John and George's shoulders.

'Will you lot bugger off now?'

*

'Running around like headless dogs.'

'Chickens.'

'Chickens. Always at us, always there.'

'Send a couple of suits.'

'Put the fear of God in us.'

'End up on the streets. Begging on corners.'

'If we're not careful.'

'If we don't watch it.'

I leave John and George and look out of the window. Everyone's gone, except for a few professionals in their various uniforms and the red-tied, white-shirted administrators, glancing up through Sven glasses and talking to each other about reaching resolution. Police and priest with their heads back. The lights start to burn out from the offices into the night. Villasocks hasn't shouted for a while; only leaves fall past our windows.

I almost fall asleep over my computer in the late afternoon, everywhere seems to settle into a slow silence broken only by computer sounds: the Microsoft sign-on, the sporadic tapping of keyboards, printers starting up. At half past five I put on my coat and follow what all the others are doing, going home as normal, though the boss hasn't said we can yet. It's only when I'm turning off the lights I remember the salesman, see the back of his head. I try to hurry by without him noticing.

'Ever been married?' he says after my disappearing body.

'Got to go now,' I say, pointing at my non-existent watch.

'You married?'

'Not yet.' I show him the keys I am carrying.

'Well don't.'

I think of Val to ease the headache, to blank Stan out. The way her hair swings as she sits next to me – hours with the straightener, she says. She says 'Hi-noo,' in the manner of some Scottish TV presenter I don't know. Her make-up doesn't quite flatten the down on her cheeks. I can see the blood working through her pale face. I'll tell her about Snuffwoman and Roofman tonight on the phone.

'Don't do it. They take all you've got.'

And maybe about Stan. I see he's been sat here all afternoon with only Maltesers, wondering what his ex-wife is up to now. He talks of when he received the divorce papers while I help him up, feel his losing-weight ten stone, the trousers flapping, the shoes with the shape of his feet worn into them. I carry his heavy equipment bag and put my other hand on his shoulder, feel the bones protruding through the material, lead him out, my second almost-crying man of the day.

'I'll be back tomorrow.'

I nod, and head down the stairs, I don't want to be in the lift with him: I tell him it's broken, 'Yes, come tomorrow.'

There's a cold sweet nag in my brain now, as though it's banana custard left in the fridge all day.

Is Val going out tonight, to that pub she took me to, or has she decided like me to have a night in with *The Simpsons* and *Buffy*? Will she laze around, smoking, not thinking of me?

Outside Jasminder and John are waiting, and we look up and around after seeing the salesman off; everyone's dispersed. No sign of cameras or TV vans. Villasocks must have come off the roof – maybe Chrissie came for him – though nobody told us.

ABOVE THE SHOP

I went round my mother's house and told her my marriage was breaking up. I was looking for some kindness. I told her the story, how things were ending, my feelings for him, his feelings for me. She winced at the word 'feelings'. I felt alone, sideways on to the world somehow. I didn't put it like that.

'Does Jeff know all this?' Her head was back and nose wrinkled to sniff out any flaws in my case. I should have known better. We were in the kitchen, Dad in the living room watching Sunday afternoon TV. I'd seen him only briefly, an acknowledgement as he shuffled in to pick up a cup of tea. His cheek – I saw only one as he backed out holding cup and saucer shakily – was fatter than ever and wobbled when he moved. To think I used to be afraid of him, his silence taken as anger when really it was indifference, his small full-stop eye never quite looking at you; now

I'm afraid of becoming like him – fat, shut up in myself. Both tendencies I have to control.

'Yes,' I said, and then, 'Don't know.' I put my head down. I moved the struggling weight in my arms. How to explain the way I saw my husband – like a pensioner pottering, or how I couldn't remember what he did at work though he had explained it to me many times.

'Don't know,' she repeated sarcastically. She had new, slittier glasses. Cup of tea steamed by the red point of her elbow, arms folded, sleeves rolled back. My elbow. My eyes too behind the glasses. 'You have to think of Tess,' she added as if I could forget her who was in my arms, interrupting our conversation with a series of bubbly sighs and small cries.

'I *am* thinking of her.' I was snapping. 'Being brought up by unhappy parents.'

She squirmed. 'How long has it been like that?'

It must have been the months of watching him as he lay on the floor – for his back, he explained – head propped on cushions against the sofa. Every night he saw the TV from below. His coffee or beer to one side of him, arms crooked back under the sofa – 'to open the shoulders' – newspapers to the other, open on the sports pages or the telly, just like my dad. Before we married I'd never seen him lie like that, unless after sex.

I first realized for sure when I found out I was pregnant and didn't want to tell him. Didn't tell him until weeks later when he took me out for a 'spin'. He said it self-consciously, twirling an imaginary moustache. In the car I felt fragile, looking across at him drive who was the father of the baby starting to unfurl in me. Things were green, lush, outside; we'd driven far out of Birmingham. We stopped for food. Even the way he walked that day, swung his arms in that baggy red and black jumper, went against him. When he went through the menu in the dark pub he pronounced the 'g' in lasagne. Le-sag-nee. His idea of a joke. I told him after we'd eaten, when he was wiping bits from his chin and picking his teeth. He smiled in relief. 'I thought you were going to say you were leaving me.' It was only some time later he patted my stomach, asked if I was experiencing food fads.

'You leaving him then?' Mum looked round as if expecting to move me in straight away (though I would never go back there), calculating the room needed, the disruption that would be caused. She frowned at me like she did when I was young. I looked away where the pan handles in neat ascending order pointed out at me from their holder in the corner.

*

The day after this I was in town and saw Dave, an old boyfriend, coming over the pelican crossing. I waited for him to see me. I ended up going back to his flat. He wheeled Tess in her pushchair through the crowds in Corporation Street while I adjusted the bags in my hands and let him walk a little in front so I could take him all in. Thinner surely than when I knew him, body bending: spine, shoulders. Wondering, too, how much I'd changed: the weight I'd put on, the lines on my face.

He lived above a shop half a mile north of the city, off a ring road, through a subway to get there. It started snowing as we walked and by the time we reached his place it was thick around us. He turned and I saw his face behind, amongst the abundant flakes. The shop didn't say what it was, just a badly painted name and number above the door. Dave said it was some kind of ironmonger's, but with little custom, cut off as it was by the busy roundabout in front. He had to catch his breath at the top of the stairs round the back after he'd helped with the pushchair, Tess asleep inside the bubble of Perspex. I put my hand on his shoulder, my first real touch, and he looked up, snow still melting on his thinning hair, with a look from way back in my dreamy youth.

His place: corridor; kitchen and bathroom right, bedroom ahead, living room left. Dark furniture, big dying plants (the landlord's). Bookcase shadowed in one corner. Dark carpet. No toothpaste (I find out later). Damp towels, a cracked window. Books on stones, history, tons of novels. He was living like a student in his mid-thirties.

Not by choice, he said. He told me, had been telling me on the walk there, how he was separated from his wife, had come back to Birmingham to escape, to 'get himself together'. She and the two kids were miles away in Manchester but he could have said they were next door for all I cared. He knew this and put on a CD and turned it down immediately, thinking of Tess, still asleep clutching Mickey, her toy donkey. He remembered – 'Come on Eileen' (my name's Elaine) – one of 'ours'. He danced – craply – to me and cleared his throat but still his voice was up an octave, and sang in my ear. He was nervous beneath the boldness, the baldness, his hand moving to my hip, but thought, because of our past, he didn't need small talk. He was right. Though the baby let out a little cry I didn't go over to check, hoped it was a small shift and she wouldn't fully wake. Then I forgot her.

*

When Jeff got in from work that night complaining about the snow, I had something to ask him. I tried to keep my voice normal as my whole mouth tingled with the lie, even inside the teeth in a line along the gum. I watched the words settle to the bottom of him. If I could go to keep-fit twice a week? You know how unfit I am, how I need a break. I was thinking of the afternoon, how we'd ended in bed after trying out table, sofa and floor, despite Dave asking that I should be gentle with him, he'd been ill. How his hands seemed to remember me despite the difference of years, the extra substance. And mine him, though he was thinner, hairier, much more breathless. How the baby interrupted us and Dave rushed across with his mobile phone for her to play with, stood to one side of her, hand over cock, as he bent to show her the buttons. How we'd shared a joint after, my first for years though I'd recently started smoking fags again when Jeff was at work, standing at the door blowing smoke into the back garden. Jeff always came in wearily, half-heartedly chucking the baby's chin then sloping off. That night he didn't say anything much, except 'You're fidgety.' Saw him thinking of the overtime he'd lose, and Wednesday was his football night (too late I'd realized that). He didn't really give me an answer. He had become a man of don't-know frowns, don't-ask-me hands. His conversation was not conversation, a series of yeses, noes and ums. I persuaded myself that I felt little guiltier about it than I did about my returned nicotine habit.

So the affair began, in January 1999. It seemed natural, a continuation, or a falling back. Our meetings were like finding days from your past coming up again, as if through some hole in history. We'd go back those eighteen years and check off all the kids we used to hang around with. Dave wanted to know if I still saw Maggie (I did – she had Tess for me some days while I visited Dave) and Liz or Ted, the crowd's gentle giant who was our talisman on our pubbing nights. He'd completely lost touch. I hadn't, quite, and had heard about others, saw their mums or relatives. We talked of the groups we listened to: Dexy's, Specials, Clash, loads of reggae – Burning Spear, or when we were feeling romantic, Gregory Isaacs. He remembered a phrase – 'What's that over there going on then?' – heard from some old bloke who'd disturbed us in the long grass at the fringe of a park – Dave emphasising the Brummie accent (he mimicked me too and I did my best to imitate the Mancunian phrasing he'd picked up). I remembered scrambling away clutching clothes, giggling, but he remembered a sharp reply, bravado. Dave liked the way my nipples still pointed in different directions (something he'd written a poem about). I told him they didn't when I was breastfeeding, which I'd had to give up due to mastitis, much to my health visitor's disgust, and had only just regained their shape. He talked of the 'cascade' of hair I had (cut now), the way it kinked in the rain.

They became more than twice-weekly visits, taking Tess with me in between. At first through the cold snap, her nose red. The importance of keeping her warm drilled into me by Mum, doctor, midwife. Here I was out in the bitter, wheeling her along the edges of dual carriageways dwarfed by hoardings, changing buses in the low winter sun, cold coming across the sea from Norway and Iceland, rolling across the UK to reach us here right in the middle.

I left supplies at his flat to save lugging them around: SMA White (on the tin a rouged baby contentedly slept); Nurse Harvey's gripe mixture; Sudocrem; Calpol; Milupa fennel variety; Bickiepegs; bags of fat padded nappies. The list is not exhaustive. Dave was sympathetic about my tales of baby fatigue, the hassle of getting ready, keeping ready, scrubbing teats, boiling bottles, Tess having bouts of sleeping only twenty minutes at a time, the feeling of having been in a terrible fight where you've had your hair pulled, your shins kicked and constant blows to the head. But don't you love her? Dave asked, and I said I wasn't convinced I did. He was good with Tess, attentive, he didn't need instructions about nappies or milk powder requirements – Jeff needed telling every time. He'd had kids of his own, he reminded me. ('What were you doing when Nelson Mandela was freed?' 'Changing a nappy,' was his response.) He missed them, now ten and twelve. Every weekend he was up the M6 to visit. He showed me their pictures; told me of exploits, adventures they'd had, minor accidents. I tried to imagine speaking of Tess in such a way.

When the weather improved we'd sometimes meet outside. On the benches around the cathedral we'd sit with the office workers eating lunch, the Goths and drunks behind us amid the graves, Tess making the pigeons fly away as she squirmed off my lap to get down among them. We didn't hold hands, but his arm was always along my thigh, the sharp-boned wrist against my skirt. I thought that when the really hot days came we could revisit the scenes of our youth: parks, canal banks, the cafés and pubs probably closed or changed. Dave took us to the West Midlands Safari Park in the old white van he picked up second hand. We all liked the giraffes, Tess included – her eyes shone as she watched their chewing heads dip gracefully to the window, and she chattered at the monkeys climbing over the bonnet. On the way back (had to cut it short because although Jeff was rarely home early, you never knew) we stopped at a Happy Eater and had burger and chips and shakes like all the other families in there.

Tess learnt to walk at Dave's, grasping his knees to haul herself up before setting off for Mickey, her nappy shaping her walk, two, three steps before she fell over. I found myself waiting for Jeff that night, eager to tell about her first steps, to show him. Jeff seemed pleased and looked at me as if I were someone new, made a comment about being different which pulled me up slightly, wondering if he could tell. I was always careful about things – showering, admitting to smoking to explain my stained breath. But Tess was developing quickly, she would talk soon and if I wasn't careful her first word would be 'Dave'. I said it so often, there and at home, changing her, holding her, dancing with her to a compilation of dance music that Dave had made for me and which Jeff mocked when he heard it one night. He sang Village People's 'In the Navy' lyrics over the opening of each track.

Dave thought of the affair as the closing of a loop, that it was meant to be since he thought he was my first. I always let him think so, but he wasn't. I lost my virginity in Woolacombe, deliberately. I ran away from my tight-permed mother and her tight-permed house, hitched back to where I'd had happiness before: a childhood holiday on the broad sands. I spent a week watching glistening surfers coming out of the sea. I was underage but went to bars that wouldn't notice. I was picked up on the second night. Spent three nights in this bloke's caravan. His moustache – the bristles brought out a rash on my upper lip – a stripe half across his moony face. A bit fat. He hardly spoke, shagged me at night and left me there in the morning in a caravan on a hillside of caravans. I don't know where he went, I never saw him on the beach. I think he was surprised when I turned up each night. He was meant to come with his girlfriend, he said, but they'd split up just before. He moaned about her after sex. I ate his Weetabix; sat in the gassy air worrying about his skill with the rubbers, thinking about the first penetration. He'd sat me on the narrow ledge seat under the cold window and knelt on something to get the right height. It hurt.

When the money ran out I hitched home. Mission accomplished. I was different. Mum couldn't reach me any more. I let her go on, her shoulders hunched behind her frown in her effort to get me to be 'sensible', let her have her say and waited for the time to get out.

Dave was second. He was then a sixth former, a bit older than me, who always got the bong out when I went round 'to enhance the fucking'. I liked his smell: some shaving foam he used, maybe. The way he looked in jeans. His hair was thick then, same deep brown as his eyes and the mole by his jawbone. He talked to me about the 'integrity of my skin', seemed to love the 'V' of my neck (he put his cock there often enough), the slope of this, the feel of that, my little toes with their 'baby nails'. Then he went off to university to study English literature and sent me pornography that he called 'prose-poetry' when he came back at weekends, less frequently as time went by.

I kept the letters for a while, twelve-page epics of lust, and gifts sent – cassettes taped, Love Hearts crushed in post office machines, the postman always demanding extra postage. Trying to keep them hidden from Mum was impossible so I carried them around with me all the time. I frequently fished through make-up, keys, photos, purse, cards to retrieve them and folded and unfolded them so many times they became crumpled, fell apart. I threw them all away when I got the final letter, following a visit when my coach got in early to Manchester and I saw him kiss a girl goodbye, one eye on his watch and how she, looking leggy and sun speckled, couldn't leave until she'd had a really good taste of him to take on her way. Actually I kept two or three of the best (reading them – the flattery and desire – was like lying in the sun) until I met Bill Smith, as dull as his name and jealous with it.

Dave wanted to know everything that had happened to me as if he had to account for every day between then and now. My work life, which was chequered and boring, clerical – council, library, health service – since I dropped out of college, while he went on to teaching, marriage, kids. And of course my sex life, A–Z, who, when, how. Men do, but Dave wasn't satisfied with summaries, wanted detail. I pretty much told him too, except for Woolacombe man: my bit of frozen prehistory. He laughed over Bill Smith with me and wondered how I always ended up with the wrong bloke. Tedious, miserly, often fussy. That was Jeff, I thought. I shook my head: 'It's a knack.'

He was curious about Jeff. I told him it was OK at first. I was in a sensible phase, getting my life on course after years of mucking about. I worked, spent money on the house – Jeff earned enough to afford one out in Hall Green – a semi with a big back garden. I worked on getting it right. Days were like things I banked to draw on later, and Jeff was great. There was a sensitivity there; he was a careful listener when I first knew him, prepared to help me unpick problems, prepared to stick around. This was a welcome change from the blokes I knew at the time. He was direct at sex, didn't hang about, which was welcome too, exhilarating, but I did come to miss the messing around. If I noticed anything wrong I put it to one side as minor. But then he seemed to get interested in work to the exclusion of all else. Probably my fault, I said, I just went off him. I told Dave about his bad back, how he hung like Jesus from the banisters, head lolling to one side then the other; how he recently had some dental problems, lost one of his eye teeth and a low whistle accompanied everything he said. I imitated him: 'Man-chh-ess-ter U-nii-ted'. ('Man U? Obviously not from Manchester,' said Dave.) How he liked to go to holiday parks even though we could afford trips abroad, liked to go to the clubhouse at night. Some childhood throwback, I reckoned. He'd get quietly pissed – though he didn't hold his drink well – and listen to the singers. Once a Jim Davidson-type comedian called out as Jeff passed in front of the stage: 'Make way, make way for Joe 90.' He was always asking after: 'I don't look like Joe 90, do I?' 'Does he?' asked Dave. 'A little,' I said.

It was only after I'd confessed all that Dave told me about his relationships. Seemingly he'd gone from me to Carol, his wife met at university (she was the one I'd seen that day), and back to me again, which made me wince at telling him about the one-night stands I'd had, taxi-ing back across the city from some bloke's flat at six in the morning, home to get dressed for work. Carol had left him and he'd fallen into depression. 'A breakdown in health. Like they have in nineteenth-century novels. I never understood that until now. Coming down here is my convalescence.' He told me that when he thought of me a calmness spread, that I was helping him recover. For me it was more fraught, the interludes between our meetings I spent like an office clock-watcher, going through the motions, telling Tess my troubles.

Once the phone rang and it turned out to be his eldest, Olivia. I heard her voice but not what she was saying, high, excited. I watched him become animated, laugh and plead for another minute or two and pledge to bring presents with him at the weekend. He put his head on my shoulder after putting the phone down.

*

Through the summer I lost him. First Jeff got ill with a cough that settled on his chest – sounded like a forty-a-dayer. Every time he's ill he thinks it's terminal, talks about what he'll do before he pegs it. 'Go see Manchester United,' who'd not long before won the 'treble' and he was the happiest I'd seen him. (Coincidentally, so was I at that time.) With Jeff at home it was one and a half weeks of days I couldn't see Dave, though I sneaked out once. Then there was the holiday – this time a hotel in Cornwall, a concession to the baby. And it was nice, Jeff pleasant and helpful and reminding me of why I first liked him, and Tess was almost speaking with the joy of crawling in the sand, but each nice day was empty. It was shortly after this, shortly after the eclipse (glimpsed in a bucket of water) that Dave said Carol had called him and wanted to get back together because she could trust Dave and not this new bloke any longer. Though he said he hadn't made up his mind yet and began to take my clothes off I knew he had. He had rung his old school to see if they'd take him back. 'They jumped at me,' he said grinning, trying to play it down, not succeeding.

*

He called me in November. Half-term, Carol out. Kids charging about in the background. 'Elaine. Good to hear your voice. Sorry I had to leave so quick. One of those sudden decisions.' 'Yeh,' I said, 'right.' 'You knew it had to end,' he said.

Propped against the back door blowing smoke into the garden, listening to the dog from two doors down bark without pause, or sat next to my husband watching a rerun of the European Cup Final, I thought about the place above the ironmonger's. I remembered the layout of the flat, so small and crowded it was like having sex in a storeroom. As Jeff watched those last-minute goals and the celebrations again, I thought of how going there was like going underwater, how I'd emerge, gasping at the daylight and people in the streets, cars parked shiny with recent rain. How the smell of the place, the years of landlord's neglect, got into my skin, along with Dave's smell. I'd always have to take a shower and Dave would hose me down like some animal waiting to be led off. I thought of the languorous aftermath, smoking together, watching the traffic flow by. I'd watch for the man across the roundabout to come out to open the doors to his pub, taking two or three drags from his cigarette and looking up and down the road before going back in – that was my signal to head home: 5 p.m. Or the evening visits when there was time to talk and relax; we played cards, flopped around listening to music. Once he got a video – *Pulp Fiction* – and after gave me a foot massage. Not a needle through the heart though.

I went back to look at the place. I wheeled Tess to the roundabout, looked across at the window where we'd sat, wondering if there was someone new there now, or if it was empty. The shopkeeper, dog at his feet, came to the door, held it half open to look at me. He chewed as he stared. Yet before, when I was with Dave, he'd kept out of sight.

It felt as if everything was over. It wasn't just me – 1999 was dragging for everybody. The feeling was 2000 should be here by now. Jeff was getting in earlier, seeming more concerned with the baby, eighteen months now, walking, talking – she repeated every last word you said – 'keys', 'or-ange'. 'Thinking of the future,' said Jeff. '2000 coming up, makes you think. Would be nice to get everything sorted, on an even keel.' I waited for further explanation, looking at his face which seemed to get rounder over the years so it resembled Woolacombe-man. He was smiling as if smiling were strange to him. The smile seemed too wide. 'We should get out more. Together, I mean.' He'd got something worked out for millennium night. Some pub on the Hagley Road, a buffet/disco ('Thirty-quid tickets!') – not a works do but several of his cronies would be there, with partners.

I found out Mum had talked to him. It was a bit of a shock. I was going to have it out with her, but found myself unable to, found myself accepting her offers to help. Suddenly I found her in my house, she who was never there much before, shooing us out and assuring us she knew how to cope with

Tess, though she looked clumsy with her. Me and him ending up at the pictures or in a restaurant like two kids on a first date, Jeff who always hated my mother now calling her 'not a bad old stick'. And he tried, it wasn't his fault, and things would be fine but then he'd speak to the waiter or something and my heart would sink. I used to think if he says the right words now, in the right order – I didn't know what they could be – all would be well, but he never did. His embraces returned too – the arms that came round my belly and breasts had a clayey, unfamiliar feel to them. I kept telling myself he's done nothing wrong. His attempts at lovemaking were tepid as if I wouldn't be able to take full-on desire. Bubbly sighs and small cries.

On the big day we watched the millenium dawn in Australia, on its way here as the earth turned. I played with Tess, tried to get her to say two thousand. She did. We put some novelty glasses on her for a quick photograph. Jeff brought out champagne. In the afternoon I popped round to see Maggie, talked about the old days. I didn't tell her about Dave, though we talked about sex, lack of it. Her husband had done a runner two years before. She's got cable, so I plonked Tess with her two in front of Cartoon Network. I drank little bottles of lager with her and wished everyone a happy new millennium. Except Colin, Maggie's ex-husband. She said I should hang on to Jeff and I agreed, said I would make an effort.

'I'll be good,' I mumbled as we got ready to leave, clenched in my party frock. Mum was making an effort with Tess, shaking Mickey in front of her, getting on her eye level.
    'What?' asked Jeff.
    'Food. Looking forward to the food.'

*

The food was crap. All hams and chickens, no good for me, a near-vegetarian. Sat with him and his work crowd, in the background a DJ played a succession of clunky end-of-the-century anthems: Robbie Williams, 'The Final Countdown'. Talk was of cars in one corner – makes and three-point turns, in-car sounds and near misses. One bloke told me how a jet engine works, how the turbine sucks air, birds into the engine, like a reverse fan. Later the music got more grisly: 'It's Only Rock and Roll' and Jeff's mates singing along, hitting the table with their fists, discussing which are the greatest pop songs of all time. Jeff was getting seriously drunk.
    None of them smoked, all shaking their heads as I offered the packet. So later in the evening, getting

on for midnight, I went outside for a fag. Anyway, I needed the air. A man was smoking there too and we smiled at each other: fellow outcasts. 'Want some?' he said. He was smoking a joint. I accepted, his fingers on mine a moment.

'What you doing at midnight?' He looked back, I saw a glimpse of his face in the light spilling out, a small nose, bigger chin. 'Staying here?'

'Nah.' But what else was I going to do?

'If we went now we could make the fireworks in the centre.'

'It's ticket only. You won't get in.' I thought of Jeff looking round for me while I ran down the wide pavements of Hagley Road, under the subway and up into Broad Street where the crowds would be gathering, music and noise everywhere. Running along as the seconds counted down, with a man I didn't know. Perhaps I could get away with it. Jeff was probably passed out somewhere by now, or would be soon.

'We could get close,' the man said. I took a drag on the joint. I knew he was assessing me by its glow: my face, my eyes, my hair. The look up and down. I handed him the joint, it was my turn to look. 'OK,' I said.

THE PARTY

His fingers play face tunes against his stretched cheek. The dead quiet of winter, the shop empty, he stands between two pyramids of yellow paint tins. The last customer asked if they had anything to make his grass greener. His boss is out the back with a salesman. Then Sue goes by. She still has that piled-up hairstyle: it needs a tiara, he'd joked. Her liquorice-dark eyes look as if the colour will leak. He watches her pass the specialist butcher's, game dangles above her. She still wears large earrings to set off her fine features. She considers the delicate set of her nose and cheeks – 'classical' someone had told her – her best point. He agreed but added the sweep of her body, thin but not too thin, smooth, when he knew her, as feathers. Like a model. Only her complexion – rosy, weathered – betrays her as a farmer's daughter.

Her second marriage had failed; a planned third had not come off. When they pass in the street he wants to offer solace, more. To embrace her strongly. Instead she gives him a quarter to three smile and he looks at her size-four feet.

He watches her go and thinks he will go to the boss's party tonight as she will be there, he's sure, looking for the next.

Whenever he sees her it throws him slightly and when he says 'Good morning' to the next customers he doesn't know which syllable to emphasise and his tunes change.

*

After work he calls in to see his mother, make her tea. He doesn't smile when he comes in, calls to her by the television, sitting in its glow. He goes straight to the small kitchen where he can reach everything: pans, tins of beans, bread and toaster, without moving his feet.

'Didun say yes, did I? Think it'll be all right to go?' His West Country accent is always stronger with her. He turns down the television and repeats the question.

'Eh?' His mother's senses are closing down, at different speeds.

'A party – I'm going to a party tonight,' he shouts. 'Go-ner live it up. Drink and dance till dawn.'

'Ah,' she leans back as far as her curved spine will allow. He examines her eyes, milking up.

'Yah'r ahl bhent up, mutha,' he imitates his boss's accent who came down from London with his own ideas about hardware shopkeeping. 'Ow long d'you fink yah'll larst?'

*

He calls in to his Friday night pub. It is Tudor: large and crooked, framed pictures of deer and lakes line the half-timbered walls. However it is low down on the tourists' lists in this town full of nodding gables and worm-rot.

'Invited to a party tonight,' he tells the barman, before taking a seat where he can watch everyone.

Two women wander in and sit nearby. Bright, dyed hair, chewing.

'See anything you like?' snaps one, red blouse, white buttons. The other, yellow blouse, black buttons, laughs. A red plastic bracelet slides over her wrist as she drains a glass of purple, medicinal-looking liquid. 'Go-ner buy us a drink?' Shaking her glass.

He looks down, grinning, and sees them reflected in the black polished wood, settling either side of him.

'Mine's a Pernod and blackcurrant.'

He buys them drinks, having to climb over their legs, jutting out from skirts, to get to the bar. They both pat their own knees to invite him their way.

They attend to him, asking questions about his job, his prospects, his girlfriends, his musical tastes. Each answer they find funny. 'He sells screws and tops.' 'He shells drills and drops.' They kick each other under the table, go 'really, really . . .' with their eyebrows raised. They egg each other on, conversing in a slang he's never heard.

The regulars do not bail him out, leer and smile amongst themselves. The barman says, 'All right there, mate,' and taps his nose each time he goes up for refills.

The yellow one, nose like two pencils, calls 'Cummon, Roland.' The other adds, 'Good old Roland.'

He is breathing noisily when he returns with the drinks.

'Puffed, Roland?'

'You misheard,' he said, 'it's Ronald.'

'Is it, Roland?'

Either side of him like flashes of colour when he moves his head. He focuses on the freckles beneath the make-up. He finds his hand, foam-rubber-like in its plumpness, next to Yellow's, he dares to catch her eyes: like dark-spotted spoons.

He could make an entrance with these two, one on each arm, sweep in, pass Sue pressing herself closer to some suit, pour shorts for his escorts and drink to cockneys everywhere. Finally he asks but gets as far as 'Would you like to come . . .' and they scream with laughter as if on cue, as if they've been waiting for this moment, and everyone in the lounge looks round.

*

He hears a laugh like it now, out on the streets. The little cinema, reopened with lottery money, empties of its few customers. There is a half-transformed werewolf grinning down from the posters. A girl – woman – walks out in front of him and he watches to see which group she will join, which boyfriend is hers. When, a hundred yards down the street, as he waits for the film-goers' cars to filter out of the car park, it becomes clear she is on her own, he hurries to close the space between them but then slows down to take in more of her walk, her body, its sway inside her pulled-tight coat. The way her hair bounces slightly on the fur collar. She shakes this black hair now and then, slips once on the damp pavement. The shape of her back is apparent, the alignment, the tapering in and out to bony hips. He keeps himself three shop fronts apart, passes his own where he stands all day amongst stacked goods. Baskets of nails, lawnmowers on plinths crowd the floors, mounted drills and cutters in wire holders on the walls. Her heels clatter like Sue's did when he accompanied her on shopping trips, always quicker than him, slipping ahead of him, through crowds.

Although it's Friday night it's quiet now the cinema crowd has dispersed. The pubs have yet to close. Drinkers on a crawl pass around him, pushing each other into the roadway. Their noise is swallowed by the next pub down. A couple wander on the pavement opposite, stop to look at lit displays of winter holidays abroad: £295, £350. A car glides by like a hammerhead shark over the seabed. There is nothing sinister, he tells himself, but he has already walked well beyond his turn off, where a party begins to blare down a side street.

THE LOOKOUT

Once I would have said we were the most visited part of the city, here at its remotest edge. Helicopters coming out of the sky, ambulances to pick up the dead and bleeding, police to take down the details. The time of Nick. Politicians arrived in black cars and walked the charred area, craning their necks to look up at the three towers perched on land that juts out into the city's reservoir. The TV crew that came to make a documentary about the crime wave had their cameras nicked. Social workers honked as they passed each other on their way in and out of the estate, particularly after 'Fanny' Adams let her daughter eat herself to death in one of the flats above us. She fattened with all the trouble around and ended up so big it seemed dangerous to get in the lift with her. Not that she came out much. Nor did anyone else if they could help it. Mugging, suicide, arson, burglary. There was an accident where a lorry came off the flyover followed by a car. Nothing to do with us, of course, but on our patch. We hardly watched them clear the debris, except for the younger kids; we were too involved in our own clear-ups.

Things are calmer now. You can't leave your door unlocked like my gran says you could in the old days, but it's nothing like it was. Now I can hang out outside (not that I do much) and watch kids rollerblade along the paths that loop down through the slopes of grass between the towers. In our block we now have regular floor parties, with all the doors open and music set up in the corridor. When the lift at the end opens by accident, the people see us and often return later. Rachel comes, the thin, dark-haired daughter of Sandy, a friend of Mum's. I call her my XYZ girl because of the shapes her elbows and knees make out of her limbs. She's rarely still, moving around constantly, tapping ash from her cigarette. You could say she's posing, but you can see she's trying things out – different clothes or make-up or hairstyles every time. She seems made for the towers, nimble, darting – I've seen her on the stairs, up them like she's on fast-forward – but able to fade into the background, essential here.

Like me. I'm nearly sixteen, little, bowed. Eyes stuck to the floor. But I see everything, everyone. From the man who lives amongst the wheelie bins in the basement and helps the dustmen and cadges fags off them, to the couple that live on the roof, nineteen floors up, take drugs and tie themselves with long ropes to the air conditioning vent in case they're tempted to fly.

I patrol. I am neighbourhood watch. Darren gave me the job. He's Mum's current boyfriend and supplies the area; not the heavy stuff, just blow, some whiz. People come and go all day, everyone calm and chatty – greeting me, my sister Melanie, seven, and Dave, the youngest, a crawler, and Darren's own – on their way to the kitchen at the back where Darren works with his heated knife and accurate scales. On nice days they sit out on the balcony and blow the white smoke into acres of blue sky they can see from thirteen storeys up (floor 12A).

Darren's never lived in a flat before and seems to like it. He points out the finer details that no one else has – the use of natural wood in a lot of the fittings, how solid and well designed the place was inside and outside, how it looked as he was driving back from one of his runs, lit up against the background of water. Most of all, like me, he appreciates the view. Mum says I spent my toddlerhood staring out at the sky, its huge rolling clouds or its far, far distances on clear days. Mum says my first words were 'fog' and 'sun'. It was only when I got older, taller, I was able to look down at the city spread below, as far as you could see, distant blocks taller than us marking the centre. I watched for signs of life: a train sliding diagonally across a corner, boats moving along the canal glimpsed through the tops of trees; closer, the flyover that looks as if it's taking off and reaching out to us but then curves away, held aloft by concrete stanchions. Darren's grateful to me for pointing out the landmarks – the GPO tower, a golden-domed mosque, the parks that are gashes of green. 'People'd pay to see this', is his verdict. Evenings are best – the sunsets (Darren and I grade them) that make the city outline look like a backdrop for a movie. And then the lights sprinkled as if to mirror the night above. When it's snowing he calls me out to look with him up into air full of smudges like ash, further up like millions of full stops.

All this is undoubtedly due to the draw he puts down his neck. I don't know what he'd be like without it. Darren smokes like smoke is air, like it is breath and oxygen, life he's tucking down there in his lungs – but he's always careful to keep it away from the kids, especially his baby (I'm allowed to join in occasionally). Mum likes this consideration, and how much of a contrast he is to her previous boyfriends, including Melanie's dad who may or not be Nick, and mine who's 'left the area' (Mum). Darren takes an interest, giving me the job of lookout and childminder, and Melanie is encouraged to do her plays, set in fairy glens with wounded horses, in front of him. He says she is going to be a great actress.

He calls me 'kid' and lies on the sofa with his hair tied back in a ginger pony tail and 'not bad muscles' (Mum) sticking out of his T-shirt. He asks me about my homework. 'Conrad? He wrote *Heart of Darkness* which *Apocalypse Now* is based on.' He retrieves the old video in its tattered case next time he's in Blockbuster and watches it with me. He loves the beginning and keeps rewinding to repeat the line: 'Saigon, I'm still in Saigon.' When Mum does have one of her mornings, less frequent now, Darren's usually there putting on the kettle, seeing to David, warming his bottle, always remarking on the broad sky at the window, having the door open on nice days although we get no sun in the mornings and all below stands in the shadow we cast, sometimes falling all the way to the curve of the flyover, its top edge across the shirts of hidden drivers on their way to work.

Mum's friends come and visit again, staying for a spliff and a chat. Doing each other's roots – there's always someone in the corner of the room with tinfoil on her head. Chatting about old boyfriends – 'There was Fart in a Colander. Remember him?' 'That bloke with hair like an orchestra conductor?' 'Oh aye, and how many orchestra conductors do you know?' Most feel Darren's good for Mum, but there are one or two dissenters. Sandy says he's too soft. 'Soft as shit. Thinks your arse is a perfume factory and we all know who's been there.' 'So does he,' says Mum. 'I don't hide nothing.'

Dave, if he's asleep, is in the pram – one bought specially to fit the lift. Melanie's in her room playing with her dolls or with one of the kids brought along, while I hang about. They've got used to my presence and sometimes talk about me as if I'm not there. 'Such a shame about his acne, will it leave scars?' 'Bound to.' If Rachel's there with her mum, which she sometimes is, I get very embarrassed. 'Still,' they always add, 'he's so clever. Always reading, writing.' 'He never bunks off school.' Then they get on to the usual subjects.

One old boyfriend always crops up: Nick. Darren, who sometimes joins the group after he's shut up shop, likes to hear stories about him. 'Was he good in bed then, this Nick?' The women differ on this, from those who knew him early – 'yes', 'strong stuff', to those who knew him later – 'crap', 'wasn't interested'.

Mum knew him early on. She was into Arnie in his *Terminator* days, and what with Nick's bodybuilding and being 'quite handsome, if a little gormless around the mouth', she fell for him. He was a new boy on the block and Mum was always quick with the new boys. He wasn't around long enough for anything really bad to happen but I didn't like him being in the flat. I tried to tell Mum but she was impatient with my seven-year-old attempt – 'You mustn't think someone's guilty because of a look in their eye.' He was obsessed with the weights he kept in their bedroom – I wasn't allowed to touch them or even look at them. I'd catch a glimpse of him sat on the bed in his athletic vest lifting dumbbells that looked like toys in his hands. He began to growl at me when Mum was out. Luckily he left for a woman down the corridor and from then on he worked his way around the block, zigzagging up and down the floors from one side to the other.

And then it began. He got kicked out by one woman too many and couldn't find anyone to take him in, not even Sandy, and began living in doorways and cupboards and spaces in the building, which would have been tolerated except he began to threaten people, write his name everywhere and throw things off balconies. He put a sweatband round his head and proclaimed himself king of the block. He threw rival males down the stairs and ran to kick them down another flight. No matter numbers. He was a gang unto himself, as police found out trying to hold him down and getting bitten and kicked. Marjory, fantastically freckled and shrunken from having too many kids or something, says, 'I'd chucked him out and he was still coming round for his marital rights even though he never focking married me. Once he's outside banging and shouting and Lynne lets him in and I tell Marcus to ring the police on his mobile. "They won't focking come," he says and I'm off to the back bedroom and get in the built-in and he's coming down the corridor with two or three kids on each arm, slowing him down, but he carries on like a focking giant, the noise he's making. I'm hid and it's like that scene out of *Halloween* with him pounding on the cupboard door and panels getting knocked in.' She's glad he's dead. Not so Sandy: 'He was bad but he had a heart underneath. Inside. He came to my door once early morning, drunk, froze, but he was polite. He had this thing that he'd made for Rachel, been up all night doing it. Tied elastic to a stick and made an elephant out of plastic and fabric and when you pulled the elastic the trunk moved. "I want to give this to Rachel," he said, he insisted and I had to get her up.' She looks at Rachel to confirm this story but she looks down and mumbles, 'Don't remember.'

You never knew what to do if you saw him, he'd spring out at you and, as Sandy says, he could be polite but would want a greeting, small talk or he became affronted. Inside knowledge helped. For instance, though he didn't like me reading stories he pored over my 'Eyewitness Account' book of big cats, especially lions. He said he wanted to fight one. He respected wildlife, he said. One day I was coming back from school, crossing the green, and saw him sat half-naked in the centre where all the paths converge. He sprang up when he saw me. Behind him the sun made scratched blinding circles on all the windows and I focused on Rachel's – fourth floor, left corner – to keep out of eye contact. He was breathing heavily, fists curled. I knew he didn't know who I was; I could have been Robocop stood in front of him.

'Nick,' I said. 'I've been thinking about those killer bees you warned me about.' (Once in a paternal mood he'd told me how to survive an attack – basically don't run.) His face changed. It was always just one emotion, in this case puzzlement, followed by joy. 'You've seen some,' he said, and his body relaxed. 'I knew it. Knew it.'

About this time Nick got into an empty flat and invited two tramps to live with him, and the next day one of them was found floating in the reservoir quite near the sofa the Fowlers heaved in the day before. The other tramp, still alive (now our basement dweller) but beaten, couldn't remember anything and Nick was shouting 'kings and warriors, kings and warriors', blood on his upheld hands. He was sectioned and finally out of our lives about the same time as Darren came along and the residents' association set up and, gradually, things improved.

We heard Nick had escaped from the secure unit and, presumably making his way back to the block, climbed into the electricity substation and electrocuted himself. The women speculate as to whether it was suicide or whether he expected to get some charge from the electric, to turn into the superman he wanted to be, and fly like a streak through the sky, stars scattering behind him.

So now I can hang out. Darren encourages me. I'm not with the cool guys, you understand, brake-driving at the far end of the grass, spraying mud at the cheering audience, but with the girls, girls who aren't cool enough to be closer to the scene. Amongst them Rachel. At the last party we stood close and moved our heads in time rather than dance together to 'I Love You Stop' which her mother, sobbing over Nick (it was a year, to the day, since his death), kept putting on, again and again. Rachel said, 'You won't catch me crying over a man.'

Now, outside, she is sneering again – up at the cars and covering her ears. 'Bloody big dating ritual,' she says. She says that in Peru the boys attract girls' attention by throwing stones at them. She can't see much difference here. I agree. I find it difficult to talk. A few days ago she was in Levis and boots but now she stands knees apparent, face like a crescent moon through the dark lick of hair that curls against her face. We talk about Darren. I tell her he's got a big load coming in today so things will be good. I tell her I've got the last of his home-grown – 'a creeper' – and we walk off round the block to see the reservoir and smoke leaning against the railings. I refrain from pointing out the moonlight and starlight broken across the top of the choppy water; instead I talk of my 'job' for Darren. How I had to know all the comings and goings as his lookout. And now you're on the lookout for me, she says. She's been thinking deeply lately and maybe I could help her decide something. 'Yeah, yeah,' I say like a Beatle, watching headlights wind up the hill across the lake.

She says come on then and climbs the rail onto the concrete lip of the reservoir. We run along it, her first, arms out like a bomber pilot. The dust and gravel we disturb tips down the side, crinkling the water. I follow the stripe of her upturned trainers. She follows the route round the reservoir to the culvert then heads inland to where the trees would hide us from the thousand window eyes of the flats. We pass the substation with its yellow 'Danger of Death' sign broken in half.

I know where we're headed. For some reason after the crash they never cleared away the car which is now part of the landscape, bushes growing up through the engine. Inside the seats are used by lovers or as a doss for those who need it or a place to sniff glue with your mates. A boy and a girl together only head there for one thing. As we get close we slow, listening to hear if someone else is there, if we could above the noise of the traffic that sweeps by above us.

'You know why we're here don't you?' she says. 'Well, I hoped,' I say. We get in through the doorless side into the back seats that she first cleared of debris. We can see the three blocks through the glassless back window. 'Darren thinks they look like those thin cigarette packets.' 'Will you shut up about him?' She makes some moves. We kiss, touch. Well, she kisses my neck but avoids my face except for one quick brush of the lips. Today she's wearing a sending-home-from-school skirt but she slaps my hand when it goes to the hem.

'You're not doing anything to me,' she says. 'This is my night. I want to see yours.' She had chosen me, I saw, of all males, because she knew I would comply. She takes out my cock and examines it like a scientist, screwing up her eyes to see in the reflected light. She feels it grow in her hand and turns up her nose. She yanks and pulls at it and peels it until I have to say careful and then 'You'd better get something.' She points it out the car but the stuff still gets on her hands. She gets out to wipe herself on the grass. I lie back.

'Put it away then,' she says. I'd been quite impressed seeing it grow bigger than I'd ever seen before, but I don't think she was. She tells me as we walk back through scrub, which in childhood I had pictured as African veldt, that she has decided, and I had helped. She was going to be a lesbian.

It's then that I notice what I should have before – an unusual amount of traffic coming off the flyover and heading for our estate. No blue lights or sirens but there are motorbikes. I tell Rachel I've got to run, she runs with me, fast as I am, faster, knowing the quickest way and leading me round dead ends I would have taken. We're still too late. We stop when we see what's happening, emerging from the wasteland. We have our arms round each other catching our breath as Darren, not handcuffed but flanked by policemen walks out and down the steps of Spencer tower. I look up to see Mum at the balcony screaming down at the tops of heads but with the noise around, motorbikes running, a crowd gathering, no one can hear what she's saying.

LITTLE CHEF

When I left John I waited until he had gone away somewhere with his TA mates. Training, yomping up hills. I packed my life into two suitcases and met Martin on the corner in his car. He was leaving a wife and kids and wanted to be as many miles away as quickly as possible.

On the drive the twitching started, as he drove he seemed to shrink back into himself. He shifted about, watching the road ahead, never looking at me, as if there was something that needed all his attention – road works, flashing lights, accidents – ahead. But it was a clear open road, a dual carriageway.

We stopped at a Little Chef; he wanted a piss, but then suggested we sit and eat there too. They were new places then, at least round here, and I was reminded of the Wimpy my dad had taken me to years before and I felt like a child again. I sat while Martin got the knives and forks and salt and pepper and sachet of vinegar. He ordered for me: burger, chips and beans like I was a child. We sat opposite each other waiting to speak and I thought he should first, he's the eldest. But the tremble he had was inside me now too and I could see looking across at him he was going to cry.

He had a shine in his eye and a throb in his voice when he eventually spoke. He said he would help with the child, he'd send me money, he'd see him/her secretly, he'd take a second job somehow but he'd just decided, on the road outside taking other lovers away, he wouldn't, he couldn't leave his wife. He was really, really sorry, he was so sorry. And he went for another piss. Why does he need so many pisses, I thought.

*

He dropped me back at the house that felt abandoned even though I'd left it only hours before. I tore up the note for John and sat and waited the week for him to come home. I went back to work as if I'd just been sick for a few days, and was sick, to prove it, in their toilet.

I resented most the stages of rejection and reconciliation I would be forced to go through, alone. I felt weary just to think of it. The trudge through those emotions Martin forced me through, the secret anger and then the reconciliation with my husband, who wasn't even aware of it. John was completely caught up in the child, Paul, his birth and growing up. He brought him up surely, steadily as I waited to love him again, and his boot camps.

I always wondered if Martin would try and see his son, as he claimed he would, turn up on the sides of pitches and shout him on, contrive to bump into us and monitor his growth, his interests, his happiness through the years. Whether or not we might meet at some function or other, and stand together and gaze out at our loved ones and others in the crowd, and slyly touch, drinks in our hands. Maybe even end up in a room somewhere, or just an alley, to get reacquainted, and how brutal and sharp that encounter would be, but it never happened. His son grew up with John; when we did meet he never asked after him, he looked away but spoke politely, softly to me about the weather or the price of houses, as if I were an aged aunt of his.

*

I remember after the Little Chef meal we couldn't turn back and had to rejoin the carriageway we'd come off, and drive to the next exit. It was maybe five or six miles, but it seemed like all the driving I had ever done and more crammed into that journey, lights flicking over us, running across us again and again, in silence, the burger taste in my mouth and throat, until we came to the roundabout and went right around and headed back the way we'd come.

AT THE BACK OF EVERYTHING

If I listen very hard I can hear the trains half a mile away beyond walls, roads and muffling trees. Julie might be on one, her gang of sixth-formers taking over the carriage. Nearer there's the road at the end, maybe that's Annie en route to work in her new Fiat. The fat glued-in homework books of her charges will slip about on the back seat. Or maybe, as deputy head, she doesn't do much marking now.

If ever I had anyone in mind, the ideal imprinted somehow years back, she was it. Knew from our first holiday in Wales, before that. But those days sealed it: lying in secret coves with her, brushing the sand and shell chips from her soles and under her toes. Her ankle in my palm. At night we entwined in our tent until we were driven off the hillside by rain, to a caravan where we listened to the radio, the rain drum, and smoked. We spent the evenings in pubs, gingery pints with dirty foam, Annie drawing men's looks. (I got used to that over the years.) Over a rickety table with Wem beer mats, under a window framing the rain-lashed bay, we said maybe we'll have a go at it. How she put it.

There was a funfair there, Seaside Terrace, and we'd go on the Cage between downpours. Annie next to me was pinned by centrifugal force against the wet metal, her hair whipped back and up, her streaming eyes crinkled as we span round. Fair, sky, fair, sky, held above the world before we plunged, to lie amongst the lights and crowds, almost dreaming the moment as I am now, lying similarly, trying to arrange my innards by willpower. My messy organs slip. Pain melts my back, or maybe the pain's not there, maybe it's my brain leaking, my lungs packing up, my heart. Something is taking me bit by bit.

*

Any day now I will be a grandfather. I wasn't told directly. Sue, who I don't see much of, thought Annie had rung me, so I didn't know for a few months. I thought she'd just got fat when I saw her, until she said, 'Well what do you think then, from the bump, a boy or a girl?' I hardly know the thin bloke she married. He has long hair, looks frail. He looked incapable of impregnating anyone, me and Annie suggested to each other at Sue's wedding. We did chat a bit. First we had that awkward moment as we met at the buffet table, she still counted calories, her not-so-new husband in the background as she said, 'Hi Phil, how's things?' A little purse of the lips at the end, almost flirty, I thought. 'OK.' I was wary but I wanted to speak, I wanted to stand once more in her good looks.

We were talking and laughing over the same things, and it was like being back in the early eighties, that easiness. For a moment I thought I would ask her back but I stopped myself in time and stuffed cake instead. I watched my daughter with her friends, pink fat arms around her shoulders, posing for cameras and strobed in flashlights. We talked then of possible grandchildren – Annie didn't like the idea of being a grandmother, felt old. I wondered how much I'd see of any hypothetical child. And now, if I survive, if I'm ambulanced out of here? I'll probably be known of, but little visited. That's how it used to be with our two. She took them with her, everything sticks to Annie.

Met her at a final-year party. 'Another Girl, Another Planet', followed by the Buzzcocks as I made my way across, drink in hand, stopped, unable to get through the crush of bodies. A group joined hands and sang the *Doctor Who* theme. Then some different music came on, some soul I'd never heard poured through the crowd, pulsed, and colours opened up to me, patterns repeating as I went over to her. She seemed bright, contained, amongst the tipped-up bottles, half-rolled spliffs and piled-high ashtrays. There was a slew of black vinyl by her feet, somebody beside her examined the gatefold sleeve of the latest Floyd album – *The Wall*, was it? She remembers Roxy Music and Blondie being on. I stood in front of her swaying. 'So you've sampled the spiked punch then,' her first words to me, a sardonic look as I stood thinking of my move across to her, through the music, my body catching up with itself, over and over. Think of it now as I bleed (or have I stopped?), coagulate on the floor, my move towards her, what line to try, what would get to her, smiling back at the people who drunkenly intervened to wish me luck in the real world. The music that started when I reached her was Talking Heads, 'The Great Curve'; I swayed over her looking down into her upturned eyes, the sober little smile.

She was in her first year, doing teacher training at the campus across town. Two years to go. I used to go across to the students' common room there, watch her talk with her mates, files on their laps, when they came back from teaching practice, exhausted. Secretly I turned down a job in London to stay around. On our first date, my exams and her TP nearly over, after listening in her room to some Bowie, hissy due to her poor cassette player, we walked down from her terraced house in Selly Oak and came across the hospital fête, and we stayed amongst its stalls. Belly dancers and flamenco out on the sports field. Some local bigwig cracking a joke over the PA system, the punchline lost to crackle. The sun seeming to take and give energy, blurring her body into the day. 'I'd like to say we enjoyed that,' piped into the air as the belly dancers finished, and the one nearest me lost her smile and looked down at the bell around her ankle. Their silky trousers billowed as they got down off their toes and walked away and Annie laughed in my arms for the first time. She glowed with a life half hidden to me. I expected to find out the rest, kissed her deep to say so, into her mouth contaminated with sausage roll.

*

I am sure I shout and shift, swear, but when I lie still a moment I sense I haven't moved at all, my blood sticks me to the carpet.

Will anyone come by? They all think I'm on holiday. Torremolinos. I've been there before, but not on my own. Birmingham-by-the-Sea my daughter, Julie, says. My case is packed upstairs, he didn't bother going upstairs: sun lotion, shorts, passport, T-shirts, a baseball cap for my balding head.

I'm just about to ring for a taxi, finishing toast, Radio 5 on for the football, when the doorbell rings. I think this is what confuses me: I think I've already called the taxi and this is it. Which it isn't. No one I know, though I thought for a minute it was Sue's ex who stalked her for a few months – she pointed him out when she visited once, stood across the road, disgruntled rather than violent. It might be the one who hangs around outside International Stores. It is: the pale face, sloping back it always seems or maybe he's just sneering at me. Teeth slope too, inwards: identikit picture I'll make if I pull through. What about his eyes? He doesn't really look at me, seems bored, I glimpse an ordinary grey-brown. Eyebrows that peter out, a nose that ends like a grape. A cut like a red stitch at the corner of his mouth. Funny thing, I'm sure he's Brummie, heard him mouth off a few times, complaints about the treatment he gets from everybody, ex-girlfriend, probation officer, God, but he puts on a cockney accent. Calls me Granddad as they do in *The Sweeney*, UK Gold, as he slides the knife in.

He has a car outside, probably not his, looks like a family hatchback, its boot up, I can see my TV sat in the back through the gap he leaves, I can see down to the road outside, no one comes along the normally busy pavement. He steps over me with hi-fi, video, looks in vain for a computer (it's at the repair shop). He already has my just-received, first-ever mobile phone, a joint present from my daughters, which they took great delight in loading their numbers on and baffling me with ring tones and texting; and the cash from my wallet. He tries to kick the bank PIN number out of me but I never use it, never look at it, every week £50 cash from the branch in the High Street. Mr Predictable. I tell him so but he doesn't believe me. He gets down to sneer more directly and I see more of his eyes then and his teeth, bits of white in a face reddened with the effort of kicking me, then he decides to stab me again, in almost the same place, for luck.

*

When I was at school Hopkins said we should all be extra kind to Helen Black when she came back after the funeral of her dad who died in an accident in his lorry up near Scotch Corner. Helen became desirable, mysterious, her eyelashes down, left alone. It was looking at her long dark hair curling, reds in it, her eyes and mouth little folds, I first felt, like a shock from an exposed light switch, what must have been love. More than lust. And then not again until that party, Annie in the corner, soberly tiddly, her toes amongst bottles and glasses. It wasn't quite love at first sight. I'm sure I'd glimpsed her once before, I was playing football drunk with all the students from the house, bored one Sunday, Penny in goal; thinking how brilliant I was to cut in from the wing, pass two dishevelled defenders but fluffing the shot, when she passed beneath trees at the edge of the park, someone like her.

Haven't felt it again with anybody, though being stabbed felt something like it, oddly, the entry of steel before a rush of pain. Poor Maria didn't stand a chance. Not Mariah, Marie or Marian, she told me on that first night in the bar. The end was there when I met her, on the rebound and she knew it too, never to stop bouncing, re-bouncing, through a second marriage and out. She called my ex 'Rebecca', after du Maurier, but Annie wasn't dead, killed at my hand – was it a gun, a ligature, or pushing off a cliff? – but living in Kings Heath (Julie: 'an oxymoron'). Near enough to bump into her in Sainsbury's pushing trolleys towards each other down the booze aisle, or outside International Stores, on the narrow pavement, people milling, the lurking stranger with the knife perhaps. Or at the cinema complex a drive away, coming out with him, bollockchops, me with Maria who steered me away, as, automatically, I headed over towards her.

*

Let me say what I want to say, says this upset caller on the radio. I hear it clearly sometimes. Mostly though it's just a hum at the back of everything. While I've been lying here I've heard Adam Faith and Barry Sheene have died. The presenter asks, 'Is this the most crucial week in history?' Another says we will be at war by the end of it.

Cars swish by outside, Shahid's car slowing down, the car that vibrates with hip hop, or is it rap, feeling into the house, along the hall as it goes by, slowly, feel the warmth of bass through the floor. Next door the other side shouting across the road to the collarless dog that runs past every morning. 'Rover.' 'Fido.' 'Blackie.' A new name tried every day. 'Charlie.' 'Bob.' Kids on their way down to the bus stop on the corner. Definitely Monday, the radio says it is. The traffic girl is speaking to me directly: soothing words about the tailback at Junction 10 near Walsall. Rain coming in from Wales. Relentless news from around the world rolling in.

Suddenly I remember lying on the carpet in front of the gas fire at fourteen years old, watching Sandy Shaw on *Eurovision*. My dad saying she would win. Her feet in tights as she did that little shuffle-dance, toes pointing in. Annie years later dancing too in her tights before going out, dancing half dressed. When she came home, that once or twice, stunned with drink, mazy, easy to manipulate, 'I'm sex on a plate, sex on a plate,' she kept repeating as I moved her arms and legs as I wished. I didn't ask where she'd been, what she'd done, not wanting to lose sight of her body in moonlight across the bed.

My sperm tasted of mustard, she once complained. It was definitely Shrove Tuesday, a drop of maple syrup on a strand of her hair. Doesn't everybody's? I asked. No, she said. She liked salt and vinegar crisps. White wine at first, until she 'grew out of it'. She watched horror films as if they were real. She believed in rapid transformation. Werewolves, vampires.

She used to say 'God created us to prove to Himself that He existed.' She used to talk in capitals. I knew her kids would love her when she became a teacher. I'd tried teacher training but failed TP. I started off confidently in most lessons, got them interested in metaphor and simile – as stupid as a coot, sir – and then some little thing, an

OHP bulb going, some large-headed boy having a coughing fit, a fart and the ensuing laughter would embarrass me. I'd turn my back for too long. The ends of lessons were always shouting at them, usually one group in the corner, a rash of them, long hair and grinning, the rest yawning, leaning back, as the noise burst out beyond the closed door along the corridor to the head's office. I switched courses, started again at twenty, you could then.

In our first flat we shared a rotary dryer with eight others, on a walled-off shop roof. The landlord put up an incomprehensible rota. Trucks the size of the houses opposite got stuck in ring-road traffic outside our window. We could have stepped out onto their roofs, considered doing so in drunken or druggy moments. We listened awestruck to our quarrelling neighbours, their detailed harangues, the uncontained anger. Her mother, on a visit watching her programme – 'Corrie', this was before *EastEnders* – said turn it down, so she could listen. Grunts and shouts. Muffled fuck this and fuck that came through. Us some years later. Not as bad, not as loud, except once or twice. Different but just the same.

I dissolve into the floor, I try to lift my head but someone has sewn my cheek to the carpet. Lilliputians while I slept. I used to read books; the night I saw her, moved across to her, I had a copy of *Zen and the Art of Motorcycle Maintenance* in my inner coat pocket, always a book in there, weighing me down on one side.

*

I'd come back from an interview, didn't get it, red tie flapping uselessly, to see him leave our house. I recognized him as a visitor to our works, where we make educational equipment and latterly software. He always wore black suits and sober ties. I was getting out of the car when he came through our gate, so different in jeans, crumpled around the knees. And her flustered response once I was inside the house, the house that suddenly looked odd to me, as if it belonged to someone else. My wife and her boyfriend eventually. He looks like a non-league goalie, big and stupid with hidden eyes, his head shaped like, and as soft as, a bollock, hair – what there is of it – like snail slime. You can understand my feelings, officer: she preferred him to me.

Him to me. I looked in mirrors and saw the set of my jaw, the lines come from what must have been knowledge of her, seeing her leave me before the process had even begun. When she went out once I searched the house and found a diary, with coffee spots and water or wine stains. Ink at a slant, abbreviations, and hints all tried to conceal what was emerging from the sentences: someone else. Liaisons after work, days taken off. I didn't say anything for a while, walked about, talked as normal, but the road I walked outside the house, with its parked cars either side, rocked from side to side, as if on a boat. I felt always soberly drunk.

The end was noisy, at times, cutlery bashing, worse for Julie and Sue, who looked on at what they'd sometimes suspected: Mum and Dad had pretended all was well, this now – arguments, slicing gestures, eyes flashing or else downcast – was what was real, was what waited for them too, just around the corner.

*

Lying here I can feel how the house works without me; wood settles, microbes grow in the water pipes, the plant tries to extract the last moisture from its mini-plot of soil. Insects and spiders chance more runs across the floor.

Work won't miss me for two weeks. Someone will call. Bound to. See through the door window, if the sun is at the right angle, through the inner door he closed, to a blurred me, on the floor, gurgling. Or am I gagged? When he knelt to check me out did he think I was dead? His face stretched as if through a fish-eye, moved back all the time, out of focus. Surely someone will come: if not today, tomorrow. Postman, gasman, salesman, thief.

*

The radio says Cheltenham Gold Cup tomorrow. Going is good. She used to be so interested in that, coming from near there, her side of the town so she saw the traffic, the TV crews and the horse boxes flowing past her door. Talked about the Irish invasion: generous, drunken, big gestures of cordiality like paying for everyone in a queue to get into a nightclub – discos in those days. The 'craic' inside with the extra money spent on drink and pills. Sticking with the winners. 'Wicked,' she said, winked at me and made me think of the night she confessed to – or did she, did I find out some other way? – how she got together with a treble-winner, an elderly Irish farmer. I imagine his rough, aged hands on her and his missing teeth, his Guinness-and-whisky-chaser belly, staying in some mid-range hotel, with him passing out on her mid-act, from the booze.

*

In a paper purple hat I met the enemy. Annie long gone by then, I was at a Christmas works do where clients were invited and there he was, a major buyer of our goods, someone to be wined and dined by my superiors, kept on the right side of lest the non-league goalie stop signing the cheques. A guarantor of my company, my job. Sat and watched him chat easily, move around different groups before we sat down. Then surrounded by smiling faces, hands on his stupid arm.

There may have been fisticuffs, I can't remember. People tell me. There were certainly names called, pushing. I waited to tell him I am a reasonable man, prepared to listen to both sides, but also I wanted to make my point, to say something, about the way it happened. I waited, got agitated, pushed through the crowd, but he moved and I caught his shoulder. He turned, annoyed, to me and whispered something like 'stupid cunt' under his breath.

I was called to the office the following Monday. I was given a second chance. I have to be nice to him, to his idea, his presence there or not at work, ditto at her house, our house, there or not, when I used to pick up my daughters and remind them who I was. The hugs and kisses, the cries plentiful at first, Julie's head lying on my chest ('Careful,' Annie said, 'she's got nits.'), Sue putting her arm around my shoulders matey-like when we parted, when I picked them up, soon fell to a peck on the cheek, a squeeze of the arm. About right considering the years gone by, the chunk of childhood I missed so that now when they appear they're almost adults with boyfriends and studies and part-time jobs and driving lessons; appearing to wish me happy birthday in the house I shared with Maria (she left shortly after their second birthday visit), to sit and ask how I am and raise a glass and say they are on their way out, some gig, hadn't I noticed they were dressed up? They'd each come as parts of couples, introduce the latest boyfriend who'd never say much, grunt hello and never give me a proper look at them, before – puff – they're gone.

*

The French holiday was supposed to be a reconciliation, though we hadn't parted. We farmed the kids out (her parents) and set off. We were going to get fit too, as well as put our marriage back together, 'get on an even keel' as she said. We were going to use the bikes we'd bought when the kids were small. We had imagined the four of us on country roads, a picnic stashed in saddlebags, a rug, fruit. But the city roads were frightening; we forgot we would have to teach the children to ride, and that seemed impossible. We ran out of patience down the park running after the soon-to-crash Sue who did learn, or Julie who never did. 'To save them from rusting in the shed,' Annie said, 'before we forget the combination numbers.' 'We can numb ourselves with alcohol,' I said, about the prospect of sleeping on grass and stones, 'cheap stuff from the local vineyards.' I knew instantly I shouldn't have said it, reviving the 'cheapskate' tag she'd given me years before when I'd suggested a few economies. Own-brand black bags for example. 'Yes sir, Captain Sensible, sir,' she said, saluting me.

The first afternoon in Bordeaux was the best, after sleeping on the overnight train down from Paris, and waiting on the station platform for our bikes, packed in cardboard and hung like carcasses, to be unloaded. We set up camp and rested, then wandered into the city and found a funfair set up in a huge car park. It seemed a good omen and we got ourselves swung up together into the air as so long before. This time we looked out into blue sky like parachutists falling backwards, clamped in against danger, padded bars against our cheeks. Afterwards we walked giddily among the French crowd, eating crêpes, or was it *pommes frites* from a cone?

We couldn't understand the language, although I'd told her we'd get by on my O level French. But they talked too fast and I only caught odd words. I always gave large notes to market sellers to make sure I covered it.

Sex only happened a couple of times in the slidy double sleeping bags zipped together. We cycled mornings along the Dordogne, following roads off to small villages which were always shut up tight. We'd sit on the village bench in the dusty heat waiting for the *boulangerie* to open. We bought by pointing and devoured the pastries outside the shop, before saddling up, rejoining the river, swirling below the road, on to the next campsite. In the evening we sat out by lakes and passed the litre bottle to and fro. At night I had stomach pangs like zips closing.

Every English couple we heard on different campsites seemed in the midst of argument. 'First you want breakfast and then you want to upset me' . . . 'because Charles is a friendly man'. With so much around us we avoided argument ourselves somehow, pretended we were French when they nodded at us; Annie looks French a bit anyway, and people would talk to her at first as if she was a compatriot. We just visited: discussed the surroundings, the meals anticipated in restaurants, next day's itinerary, we pored over the unfolded map, eating St Emilion macaroons. The prehistoric caves at Lascaux were shut; we laughed at the crudely done statue of prehistoric man, complete with club, on the hillside opposite. We reached Sarlat: the photo of her pushing the bike up cobbled streets, beneath gold stone towers. But we decided to turn back before we had to tackle the steep inclines of the Massif Central: not fit enough.

So it wasn't going badly when I became ill, feverish, with dreams of the sort when you peel an orange to find a peach. I didn't tell her how ill I felt on that long ride to the beach at Arcachon. 'We have to see the sea,' she said, 'I miss the sea on holiday.' So we changed our plans and headed straight west, down the long straight road that rolled out through pine forests, me feverish. I had to stop to catch my breath, hunched in a little clearing, while red squirrels, almost black, scrambled up fir trees. Annie stood in shorts by her bicycle, leaning now and then to try her brakes, test the gears. I made it, prickled with sweat, to the disappointing beach, couldn't go any further to discover the better ones, dropped onto it, a small yellow strip beyond mounds of greasy seaweed. I lay in pain, in fever, in the yellow hazy heat. Boats on their sides were floating when I next looked. The sea when it came slid in, smelt of decomposition and crept to our feet with weed to deposit. She said far from reconciliation it was where she decided to leave me. On that 'beach' with no cafe in sight. Me running a temperature and moaning about being thirsty. That's not fair, I said, I was ill. 'You're always ill when it matters most,' she said. I don't know where she gets that from because I hardly miss a day at work, though I'd like to, I'd like to pack it all in now, I'd like to pack everything in now.

*

If I could see Maria again, now, I'd ask if we could try again; the more I think about her, lost to my moods, and hardening, the more I think how I wasn't good for her. I could make it up to her now, take her out and woo her again, try my best, be fun and attentive, like Cary Grant, maybe. It could work; it could because I'm over Annie. Now. I see now I was preoccupied, see her point now. After the works do I had a bit of explaining. Maria said she couldn't compete with that. After I'd got used to her about the place, who herself was beginning to look comfortable in the house, making an impact with plants and pictures, brightening up its old furniture with new cushions, introducing new dinners and ideas for holidays, Maria slipped away.

Since then, the single life. Bananas and toast and espresso for my evening meal. I indulge, binge: beer, crisps, chocolate (wrappers fill the bins), porn. Endless porn on the net if I want it, but I find myself longing for the days when it was stumbled across, rare, through a friend who'd been to Germany. Brown paper-covered mags sent off for. Then I'll do nothing, not bother, not bother cleaning, clothes lasting a little longer than they should do. I'm getting clumsy too (old age?) – a plate smashed, a jar of Marmite cracked and splashed on the blue-tiled kitchen floor.

Single, but one-night stands now and again. Oh, there was Lydia, almost fifty, but pretty still, in the eyes, still clumped about in platform soles I hadn't seen in years. Her bracelets shook as she moved around my house, bringing in a meal of fish and chips and transferring them to plates. When she walked she leant forward stiffly from the waist. A couple of months then, I admit, with her. She didn't move in, she visited. She was a widow, her kids grown up, reliving her youth. She said after a bout on the sofa that she had got glassy, locked up, shopping in supermarkets in a dream. She liked me, the sex offered, and then it was off to do her shopping. Less glassily. She stayed one night only, and that wasn't planned, she just got too drunk. She showed me a picture of her and her husband: she had a striped blue dress on, and he a mustard shirt with braces. They looked a different generation to Annie and me.

*

Julie stayed with me for a couple of weeks when Annie went into hospital (for minor surgery – Annie didn't feel the need to tell me what) and loverboy was jetting around the world no doubt saving our company, making deals and consolidating profits. Julie was eleven, less than a year after I'd gone, and acting as if it was normal to go away for a while, then return. It was her clear features, the freckly complexion I revered, exact and uncomplicated. I gave her sweets. She liked soft ones, sugar coated to melt to flaps caught in the teeth. I made her eat her tea, though, is that a palindrome, is it that, is it that, can hear that beat again, slowing, a majestic pace to it, blood slowing down, about to stop.

I'd take her to the park, play footie. She would be goalie, and I'd try to score. I gave her easy shots, praised her catches, bowing before her holiness in the end. 'Don't be silly,' she said, but once I'd managed to pucker up that smile I'd try and keep it there. Sang, danced, told bad jokes involving elephants in trees and multi-storey carp arks. I mocked her teachers. Once I reduced her to helplessness, she held me tight, splurted laughter. Then it was my turn and I let in outrageously simple goals, let the ball slip between my fingers. There she was, always within the distance of my weak throws, weaving a geometry of chase and return.

The wind smacks the window. I want to go to my beach in Spain, ignore the timeshare sellers, the drunks with Union Jack shorts, the topless brown bleached blondes, even them, walk down the pathways between the strips of flowers, past the shops with revolving racks of postcards and soft toys and plastic souvenirs, and get to the beach. I could be there now, day three of the holiday, smoothed out, glowing from the sun. See my tanned arms on the table in front of me in the taverna, glass of cold San Miguel releasing slow bubbles beside my hand. If I'd left five minutes earlier. Then maybe he'd just have burgled, he didn't want to kill me. But he rang the bell.

The bell is ringing. Someone looms, their shadow on the glass, broken up by the pattern of the stained-glass border, a 'feature' of the property, said the estate agent; now I wish it was clear. Circulars and pizza menus float down from the clanged slot. Now he's rung next door, I can hear them talking on the doorstep. The woman's laugh comes under my front door to me, I picture her from her laugh, her whole self reassembled around it, she looks down at me and extends her hand. She takes the parcel and goes in, slams the door so it shudders, I feel it send pain from a wound I didn't know I had, just in from the hip.

*

There was a time I saw my kids daily, almost, picked them up from school and drove them to his house, our house, and waited until their mother returned. Her blouse was always crumpled: marks of the day, ink daubs, sprinkles of chalk dust, paint-soiled water spills. We spoke little as the kids told her of their days. Sometimes I felt shy as I opened the door, kids ready, to her. As if she was a possible future lover, not an ex-wife. She talked briskly, didn't look me in the eye much, unless to get crucial times and places of next meetings, kids' outings.

I laugh like a horse at something on the telly. Why is the TV in the hall anyway – didn't the robber take it – and why is it twice its size? It blocks the way, someone's breath comes out of the curved screen as he is murdered. He falls to dumps of slush in the streets. Can't I hear the kids laugh, the sea lap on the radio behind the reasonable voices, the sound of this drama?

I feel nothing more than rubble. I slump over the pain; I could do with food now, a glass of water. A fag even would somehow help, even though I haven't smoked in years. The smell of rain comes under the door, or the smell of corruption. Am I decomposing? The buzz of a fly is like a little machine as it flies past, low enough to feel the wind of it. If I lie here long enough I'll attract insects and rodents from around the street, through the drains, airbricks, skirting and floorboards, slugs and mice and spiders and rats.

The air under the door wants to enter you, to get at your blood and sinew. It smells like a crop of boils, smells like him, like pus, like poison, like the sea lapping, weed choked. Blood is dried in rings around me, and piss/shit too, pisshit, smells like a headache, the rain under the door. I make one last effort to scream, to shout through my caked mouth, and feel the rip in my throat.

The air is plastic, stuff fills throat and lungs, nose and mouth. A tearing somewhere, people hit in shadowed corners and falling. Sometimes I spiral up to a whiteness, a blankness, no names being called, nothing. There breathing is easier, but the air is not right, somehow crumbly in my lungs. I recall moving. Across that room again, legs moving, I remember that, moving, across the music-blasted room to her, held in the arms of a dark green armchair, next to that guy sorting through records, waiting for me to come along.

The door breaks above me, air rushes in as if it had been sealed out, a big square of air, it bruises my eyes with its touch of glass. I hear wood rip, and shouts, crackling radio voices, bleeps. Air carries me off, or men lifting me on a stretcher, the ceiling shifts down, a whooshing sound comes from the hole in the side of the house where the door had been. I'm carried on air, lifted, outdoors; the stars are suddenly there in the strip of sky between house and ambulance. Blue light is flung around the street as it waits, doors open, in the middle of the double-parked road. Between the house and the ambulance I let go. I'm on my way, floating, shimmying, over rooftops. The world below upends.

BACKGROUND NOISE

1

When J. said – texted – come to his place in the city I was glad of it because Manda was on at Mum to chuck me out anyway. She would have done it too because she does everything Manda wants. The trouble between us was sex of course, me with her boyfriend, who was useless anyway. The opposite of J. It just happens, I said to her, Sloppy Pete was drunk and horny and so was I, and she sneered, 'Irresistible, are you?' and called me the usual, and immature as well, when she's only nineteen herself.

I'd met J. in a pub, didn't know he was lying low then. I was with 'friends' in the hometown, kind of a reunited thing, a year after school. He was on his own in the corner. He didn't respond to our bantering (we all instantly fancied him) but I could see him watching us, and how he zoomed in on me. I felt his stare on my neck and below as I drank. Later I found him walking me home. The sex was good, considering the booze; he took his time. He took my number.

He visited me a few times and then phoned and emailed when he went back. He sent me pictures of his cock, said it was pining for me. Then the text inviting me to move in, help him settle in his new place, just when I'd had enough of Manda.

So I packed in my first ever job at the dentist's, packed what I had and came here where there are no fields. Just runs and runs of grey houses, criss-crossed with roads. I was fine for a while. I walked to the shops and bought stuff, I met people to say hello to, I read the new graffiti on walls and bus stops. On one terrace end, some artist had come and spray-painted a beautiful, larger-than-life lion. The lion stood and watched people pass, a pride in the background. All the forest leaves, his mane, were flecked with painted yellow sunshine.

I got used to the life here, his friends who come round and stay for days, clutching bags of weed or pills and stolen mobiles and bags and boxes of electrical goods that pile up in the kitchen. Doing them all Pot Noodles or handing round delivered pizza. For real munchies, marshmallows and ice-cream, Magnums of course, but they like different ones: almond, classic and white chocolate. They show me their scars and muscles. Their new tattoos: flames and women and knives. Their just-nicked Nikes. None of them seem to have girlfriends. It is never said but it is clear J. is *the man* around here. He always gets first hit of the bong, first swig of the bottle, his opinion on football and music sought. The instigator: he'll lead them to the offie and keep the assistant busy, smiling, interested, while the others work among the shelves. Even when he was temporarily crippled in a fight, on half crutches, he'd be stood in the centre of the room, doing a Scottish sword dance imitation, pointing his bandaged foot, or 'shakin' all over' like old people. His torso and arms shown off. His men grouped around him smiling and stamping their feet. I sit back too, on an E usually, and admire him, the strength that could pick me up like I was a cat, his fine-cut face that can't yet grow a beard, something else I like about him. He looks Swedish or something, high cheekbones, not blonde though, well-cut brown hair, good through my fingers. He flicks me smiles. I bask in the attention I get, from him and them. He has me sit on his lap while he talks through the latest plan, what they should do next, who should do what, and seems to like them looking at me with his hand on my leg. He says later he plans to video me with them, spice things up a bit, it's sex talk to get himself going, he says he'll get another girl in, but I've never seen another girl.

I sit next to him while he plays mind games with some of them like Terry the geek with the long twisted face who tampers with the mobiles to make them resellable. J.'ll ask him about his ideas, 'Let's hear yr flossophy,' he'll say imitating the way Terry talks, handing him beer and spliff. Then he'll encourage him while Terry twists his legs and tells us all about computers, war and mathematics. How everything comes down to a number or a set of numbers.

'Really, professor,' J. will say, pressing his leg against mine, repeating part of a conversation we'd had in bed, how he'd get Terry to this point again. 'Twelve, twenty-four, forty-eight?' Him saying those numbers deadpan will make me snort the laugh I'd been holding.

J. himself, though, if on the right drug, will talk of how he sees things. There are rages in the universe, and their ripples hit Earth. That's tornadoes, volcanoes, hurricanes, but they're also inside you, they go through you too, you can feel them coming. He says we are microbes, germs and our little rages, the violence we create, are nothing.

As if to prove it I saw him beat a man once. I was out with them in some pub on the outskirts. The man was big, unafraid and picked on the youngest of our crowd, still at school. After all we were on his turf. Didn't worry J., who set about him with fists and feet and a determination that won through, the bloodshed not bothering him, nor the pain. He had cuts and stuff but it was the other one that limped off. I licked J.'s wounds after.

He will talk a lot some nights and I like it because we get undressed and get to it slowly, we slow it right down and try to get our blood to go round in harmony. The drug lets us hear our blood course like tiny streams inside us both, and we listen to get our different flows synchronized with each other and the music we play, then we slowly fuck. Everything then feels good, right: he is in me and around me, he seems like me.

After, if he hasn't gone to sleep, if different drugs kick in, he might talk of what he will do, how he'll give up robbing one day. Stop sending me out shoplifting. Lower the amount of drugs; get a job, a proper one. He even talks vaguely of having kids eventually.

*

Things you wouldn't dream of doing – shoplifting, having near-sex with him in front of his friends, stealing from your mother, or your virtual mother,

her online account (you guess the password is Manda's middle name) – you end up doing as if in a dream.

I'm one of the gang, though I don't go on the big jobs, the more-than-one-day jobs. I shoplift in Boots and Woolworths, the old shops the easiest, bus trips to the centre in the big coat he gave me especially for the job. I move through the shoppers quietly, I could be anyone. I come back with stuff like the rest, some sellable, some for the house, ornaments for the sideboard that get broken, and we, me and him, or a whole crowd, crack open booze and get the drugs out.

I've got an eye for the put-down iPod, the open bag. I spot open windows, report back when I see a family load up a car for holiday. I notice alleys and doorways and gates set back from the road where you could hide or wait. I break into neighbours' houses (flats are better), slip the catch like he showed me, to see if they have anything lying around: cash, mobiles, laptops, DVD players. It seems like my own decision.

But when he's away on jobs for days the house noises lodge in my head. At night it creaks and groans like a ship at sea, how I imagine a ship at sea. In the day there are the neighbours through the walls or out the back, giving me the evils as I come and go, or the wind down all the alleys moaning and whistling. Sometimes there's nothing, no cars or calling across, no taps running next door, no strange humming that comes down from above, no shouts or dogs, nothing, and I try and have a drink or a smoke to enjoy it more, and think back to the quiet of the hills folded around where I came from.

I'm never sure which drug to take when on my own, and take the wrong one, the wrong colour, the wrong shape and end up shaking in corners, or crouching on the floor, holding myself in. I've learnt that it ends but until it does anything, the sound of ash dropping into coffee, the spill of goods and packages in each room, putty fingerprints on the window, will set me off. I can't put the telly on because the news seems to be my fault: the wars, starvation, bombs, people burnt, the missing and murdered, all because I didn't pay enough attention, I got myself distracted somehow.

*

We once visited his family across town. He usually didn't want to but something forced him across the Sunday roads, driving as if to catch up with himself (we would have a car and then we wouldn't), checking his chin in the rear-view mirror, checking my legs sliding on the seat. I couldn't find a seat-belt.

The family were all sat out the back, as it was hot, though it was March. I could see through dusty windows into their living room, on a wall-mounted screen huge statues of Buddha were blown up like unwanted tower blocks. His mother stood at the back gate, black hair forced back, her mauve top rolled up to just under her breasts, griping loudly to two women in the lane behind.

A man, who looked like J. might look in ten years, his hair beginning to fall out, dominated one conversation. As at home the others grouped around him holding beers and fags and turned to spit in the waist-high hedge beside them. 'Imagine: twenty grand in five minutes. Right, you're saying, great, go for it, but you've got to take into account the downside, haven't you, the possible downside . . .'

J. tapped me then and turned me round and kissed me in front of them, did a kind of Latin thing, *Strictly Come Dancing*, bending me back and making sure they all saw where his hands were. Whistles and shaking of heads. One of them came up after with a drink for me, bowing like I was royalty, so I could see the stitches in his bald patch.

Later an argument, a bit of pushing around, was broken up by a voice from an upstairs open window. The father, or grandfather, who I hadn't known was there, continued to shout out now and then. Orders for drink or food, and comments – I apparently was OK, better than J.'s previous, and would have to meet him later, but J. got me out pretty soon after that.

That night I tried to picture my family while I listened to J.'s thick breathing. It was hard to get the pictures right, they all got mixed up. My mother's head – her dyed dark hair, her lined mouth held tight – on Manda's neck or the other way round. I pictured them not missing me.

*

He has jobs sometimes, some kind of benefit problem otherwise, night shifts at the shopping centre, or something in a factory, but he always picks a fight or refuses to do something, and gets sacked and comes home again. Can't stay away from me, can't get enough of me. He comes home with his cock ready. His cock: I look forward to seeing it again each day. I like to hold it in my hand while I fall asleep, feeling my grip go. Or else hold him in tight after sex and feel him shrink inside me, and then revive. I don't like it when it isn't working properly, when the drugs are wrong.

Sometimes I have to remind myself why I like him, he does such weird stuff. Something gets into his head and that's it. Like pushing the furniture around and into unlikely places, an armchair squashed in the under the staircase cupboard. He tore the gas fire out with his hands to put in a coal one, he said, but left the hole instead. Pots of paint will line up against the walls but nothing gets painted. He'll write things on the misted-up mirrors in the bathroom, hard to read when I go in, the letters running with condensation: something was coming, the sun would dim.

I took to sunbathing to get out, to feel light and heat on me after the dark cool house. The summer started off warm and got hotter. 'I'm going to get brown,' I said. 'Would you like me brown?' He watched me take the red recliner out, never offered to help. Watched me instead from an upstairs window, told me he was thinking of what the neighbours could see from their upstairs windows, 'watch your flesh frying,' he said. They'd see my bikini-ed form splayed out amongst the paving stones, the tufts of grass, my freckles slowly merging as I went red first, then tan under the sun cream.

*

For my birthday he took me to a Beefeater; he hated dealing with the waiters though and I had to order. I chewed on the steak he insisted I had, saying how he liked it bloody, with mushrooms to mop it up – he put some proper shrooms in it too, when it came. I watched a family behind his back settle around a table with menus and napkins lined up. They were like mine in that there were two girls, but a lot younger, and there was a father too. I watched them talk together quietly, just above the old music from the PA – 'You Don't Have To Say You Love Me', sang a woman – and they offered each other tastes of prawns and bites of steak on forks, and touched each other's sleeves for them to look, look at what Betty or Jill was doing. The waitress to one side took down their wishes. There were paintings of mountains behind her. I watched all the courses arrive and how they smiled when each came, especially the creamy desserts. J. wanted me to suck on my banana split, give a demonstration to the people in this warm brown room, under mock chandeliers.

2

I come in through the front door after an unsuccessful shoplifting trip, it's too hot for the coat, and I know there's something up, there's another smell about, and, alert, like I'm on a break-in, I open the front-room door quietly. There's a man smiling, but I know he's dead straight away. He's sat in the chair staring at me but underneath his shoulders are all wrong, the angle. He's got a colourful tie on I thought was spilt blood at first. He has a little moustache, ginger, grey at the ends, and as I'm looking his chin sags and his tongue is black.

Then J. comes in, looking hot, and as if breathing water. Gurgling, almost. He's got a cloth laid over his arm, carrying our green bowl, steam coming up, he's concentrating on not spilling it, and for once his arms look weak.

'Ah, you're here,' he says, 'just in time.' Trying to keep his voice normal, a cough leads him there. 'Here, take this.' He nods down to the cloth.

*

Two Jehovah's Witnesses knock on the door during our clean up and I answer mopping my hands, the clean, iron smell of blood up my nostrils and in my mouth. They have leaflets illustrated with children hugging lions and a feast of fruit on a table behind them. The older man, with a white patchy beard and eye whites that are grey puts the leaflets in my hand and I feel the calluses on his fingers brush my palm. I wonder they can't smell the blood, and when the dogs passing will head for here.

J. comes and stands behind me while I see them off, listening to what I say though he sent me to the door in the first place. All I manage anyway is 'No thanks, no, no, no thanks.'

*

The reason he killed the man, he says, is because he wouldn't go away. Some kind of won't-give-up salesman who somehow got inside while J. was on the crest of a high, thinking he'd got his foot in here and sat down and got out his glossy brochures for gas fittings and fireplace surrounds, looking with joy at J.'s unfinished hole in the wall. 'How about a whole new central heating system?' and J. says he was stood in front of him, 'my breath going in and out wrongly'.

'My head started to flip with it. I went and got that.' He points to the remains of a paving stone scattered around the chair, on the man's lap. He brought it in from the yard. It's the one that I put my romance books on when I sunbathe. A thick triangular chunk of grey on the carpet has a circle made by my Coke glass.

The sun must have been beating down in my corner; he must have lifted it with difficulty, even with his strength, and carried it in as the visitor rummaged in his briefcase, waiting for his return.

Before the ginger man could speak, or maybe he was talking into his briefcase, J. swung the slab one way to gain momentum – he shows me, twisting his torso round, his cheekbones catching light that comes in from the back – and then round across the head, the bent neck, taking bits with it and grinding grey and yellow flakes of concrete into the brain matter.

'He got up almost completely,' J. says, 'turned to carry on the conversation, but then sat down again. So I just banged it down hard on his head from above, like this. Until it all broke up.'

'I made him go away,' he says. 'Only he's still here.'

*

We move him, chair and all (most of the blood has soaked into the chair), into the cleared-out cupboard under the stairs, its old home. He just fits in sideways but I have to get into the space with him, J. is too big, to move him in enough to close the door. Head to head I see close up the ginger in wavery lines in his moustache, the neck chafing at the collar, the concrete dust and bits in his hair and clothes, one large pink and chunky ear split in a V, the fillings glint in his blackened mouth while I push and wiggle the chair, having to bend right into him. J. pushes from outside. A sour – or is it sweet? – body odour comes up from him, any deodorant he may have worn worn off. He seems wet all over, soaked in something invisible. Or perhaps it's me – I have a sheen of sweat. I know it would look good in a photo, the sweat highlighting my tan. My hair drops all over the baldness I never saw at first, him getting first view of my wet neck and tits, blouse open to his dead eyes. He has grey and ginger little stripes, more orange, the colour of fish fingers, in his irises too. I push him to one side accidentally and his head that seemed stuck with the blood leaking into the chair goes forward and I can see more how the hair frames a deep jagged wound, a gap as big as a baby's fist, and mixes with the little cuts and wide red scratches greyed with dust. Flesh bits, concrete bits on his shoulders. I put his head back when I can and he looks like he might say something and I can picture him talking and wonder what everyday phrases finished him off. J. says he probably didn't know it was going to happen until it did.

*

I miss my old job, even miss the bus journey through fields of wheat, past hills that swept down to the roadside, ponds glimpsed within coppices passing.

I miss trying to ease the nerves of the dentist's patients, or slotting them into appointment diaries. It was up to me to soothe them after their surgeries, 'Oh yes, that will be like that for two hours now,' or speak on the dentist's behalf, 'Mr Downing likes to follow up quickly. Next week at the same time?' I answered their hard-to-hear questions, mumbled through anaesthetic; I'd smile at them and bring them down to calmness.

I liked to speak to the dentist on the internal phone, listen to his phlegmy, deep voice. He did things a dentist isn't supposed to, smoked and ate spicy food deliberately to breathe over his patients. 'They've got no other dentist to go to,' he told me during a break out the back, 'captive audience.' I think he was building up to ask me, you could see it in his little leery glances, and despite his granddad age, or because of it, I would have, probably, just to see, but then I came here.

*

J. tells me to go out and get some fags after I shower and change, he was going to think what to do. I don't know whether he is testing me to run away or go to the police. I walk down to Imran's how you might have anyway if you hadn't just helped tidy away your boyfriend's murder victim.

Things aren't the same though: the people that pass seem like things about to sting, like stinging red substances walking, booted and belted. Each car that passes in the burning day seems to carry off a piece of me, caught in an open side window or behind a wiper, shreds of me going from here to all over the country.

In the shop I get out money and pay. The woman with the whisper of beard and wrong-looking glasses knows what happened at our house, can see the body in my eyes, the under-stairs, but takes my money anyway. Her face has lines within lines that I only now notice after months of coming here. I want a closer look. On the way out the shelves bend over as I walk by, but all the goods, the stock, the bars of chocolate and chewing gum and the tins with marker-penned prices on them, the little jars of coffee and rolls of biscuits and bags of Bombay mix stay still as if glued on. Then they do up like a zip behind me.

Out on the street the pavement burns up through my trainers. The lion watches me with disdain. A couple of lionesses from the pride get up and pad out through sunshine from the bricks. They don't roar. I run a bit to get out of their sight. I think about ringing Manda when I stop and even get the number ready – she won't recognize who it is on this stolen mobile – just to hear her voice ask hello, hello.

I should just walk the other way, down the side street to the junction where I can get a bus to the centre and catch a train, a train anywhere, not back home, and start again and be happy ever after without him. Get a cat or something, give up men altogether, sit at home and sing to myself.

*

I say when I come in, 'The sun has beaten me today,' examining the freckles fused now together across my shoulders and arms. At last the desired effect – I am a polished brown, richer looking, all touches of red disappeared. 'Eaten you,' he says.

He fucks me a lot through the rest of the day and night, on the sofa, missing its partner chair, the telly showing a riot going on not two miles away. We watch the cars on fire, the lines of police. J. says something about it being the ideal way of getting rid of the body – a riot victim. 'There'll be a few murders tonight.' But we don't have a car to drive him there. J. says he'll get his cousin to bring over the van later and I think, what about Stan's car, he must have had one.

I call him Stan, Stan Hodges. I could find out his real name, go through the briefcase on his lap for business cards. His wallet has been emptied of money and put back; J. did that, his wedding ring pocketed. J. is wearing his watch even though he describes it as crap. I think Stan Hodges has two kids who sat on each knee when they were small and he kissed their heads, their cheeks, and they complained about the scratchiness of his moustache, not grey at all then.

J.'s cock stays big for hours, I'm not sure if it's because he's taken Viagra or something similar or if it's a side-effect of becoming a murderer that afternoon. During it, the long night of fucking, I think of how I might be mistaken, and that there is no one missing the man at all. How he was a loner, a divorcee. A widower, maybe. How no one will report him missing.

But I'm sure by now his grown-up kids with ginger and grey eyes, responding to their mother's distressed call, are organizing search parties to go looking for him – Stan Hodges, who saw them through university, who liked bright ties and country walks, and when he was younger went to the movies every week with them both, sat through every Disney and always remembered birthdays; through the night they'll look for him, before going to the police.

RIVER WALK

By the weir the river widened, went off to a lock one side, the water tranquil before, still almost, poured in a long thick sheet over the round edge to crash in foam. He followed the path up watching the water's whorls, glints of sun, the sticks, ducks and boats upon it, a matchbox coming apart. The wide bank mud whitish-brown, cracked into lozenges. Moon daisies were sprinkled amongst huge strangling buttercups.

He set off down a footpath away from the river, close to woods, and something drew him in, ducking under scratching branches, on inside. They were inside a knot of flowers and trees in a bush-filled clearing, seen through dancing shadows of leaves and tiny splashes of yellow sun along her thighs, her skirt pushed back and squatting so her knees were either side of him, stood above, his cock out, the erection lowered to her opening mouth. He looked away, turned away, quietly went off like a mother leaving her sleeping child, whereas he thought he'd wade in with stick or brick, crash in with noise and thunder, but instead went out of the wood watching his feet, thinking of her eyes looking up to him like that. Her T-shirt rolled up, her bra too to liberate the breasts. He had seen the penny-brown nipple show when she lifted her arm.

He walked back along the river, his heart erratic. He heard the wet flap of a bird taking off, watched a family of ducks close to the far bank follow his progress. Above them thistle seed floated heavily off in waves.

*

He got to the hotel room and drew the curtains in their room, and wondered how long she must have planned it. The cleaners knocked then and he let them in with their trolley of towels and sheets and went and sat in the bar, just opening, to wait for their lunch appointment.

*

He didn't know how he managed to speak, pulling the dried-up tongue from the roof of his mouth, when she came back and touched him lightly on the arm, saying she couldn't find anywhere selling the walking boots she needed. All the shops were shut, she said, curling her nose in disgust at the closed Sunday countryside. Even the nearest big town which she'd driven to didn't seem to have what she wanted.

They ordered lunch, the ploughman's that she laughed about – you know they made this up, no such thing as a ploughman's until the seventies.

When she said she would probably go looking for boots again tomorrow, that there was no need for him to come, better well-shod if we're going to tackle those hills, he got up and left. He did mutter 'toilet' on his way out to the street.

The few people out seemed to be halfway through things – getting into a car, doing up a shoe-lace, about to cross a road. He went down the lane between the shops, where the half-timbered dwellings behind tumbled down to the river. Up ahead a boy with white shirt hanging out crossed a bridge. He could hear the mill nearby, a constant churn, sound reversing into itself.

He passed along the wet footpath by the river, and away from it along a tributary, a brook, little red mushrooms at his feet, pushing through the mulched leaves, feeling his soles press acorns and caterpillars into the ground. He passed under the curve of a hill not worrying if it was a footpath or not, climbing over trees with their roots hanging over the water, past a patch of bright spongy grass they might have used for a picnic.

On another more distant hill he could see a red wrecked tractor gliding in steady undulation over a black oblong surrounded by green. The hum of the vehicle seemed to come from behind him, loudly filling the air at one moment, tinnily distant another.

Then more thickets and retraced paths to get through when his battering didn't succeed, the brook dropping away as he climbed steadily up, the sweat salting thin wounds. Sometimes he heard human voices like a party about to begin somewhere.

His phone went off in his pocket, startling him with its three-tone song, and her name on the screen. He looked at it, her name in his muddy hand and the thing vibrating his fingers and he hurled it like a cricket ball over the ridge towards the brook below but it didn't reach and landed in a bush where it continued to ring, and he went quickly on. It was a long time before it stopped and then he was on the other side of the hill panting, ready for the run down it when he heard it again. He ran down, tripped, rolled, mud collecting, coming to rest against a boulder where he stayed and listened to the afternoon wheeling around him, the birds scratching the air and some motorway, way back, constant, and only got up when he noticed some walkers about half a mile away coming up from a car park below.

*

He hit road, a muddy lane, and a horse passed, the flank near his face, that skin over bone and muscle, the clomping and breathing of it, the leg of the woman. Up above someone looked down at him, saying something, going by ponytail and horse tail swishing in time, retreating.

The smell of a sewage works brought him to the outskirts of a village that had a station entrance on the road. As he reached it he saw a train there on the single platform, its doors open. They closed as he got on as if the train had been waiting for him.

He sat by himself on the scratchy plaid seats, the local railway's logo on the window he looked through to see the station slide by. There weren't any other passengers, but soon a conductor showed up and took his money and then stood at the end of the carriage and looked at him, hands on his little machine of tickets and pouch of money.

There were several stations and people got on but avoided sitting next to him, seeing the mud on him, or maybe the eyes that seemed blank but waiting to be angry if anyone touched him or made him move.

He got off at one, in the suburbs by now of some city, got out on the busy platform, people moving out of his way and going through a gate onto the canal that ran alongside the line. He followed the straight line through factories with their backs turned, chains clashing inside, saws with their glittering screeches, the chug of motors. Then wasteland, armies of lupins rushing at him, patches of gravel and puddles sparked the towpath. Every now and then a train would speed by and people going miles away would spot him below walking the same way but rapidly left behind.

*

In the back of a canal pub a man reading a newspaper next to him nodded and showed him a report about robberies in the area. He drank and lurched down corridors as everyone does in pubs. It was one of those pubs that meander about with half-closed function rooms, doors leading off, a staircase going two ways. He glimpsed the woman in one of the rooms, maybe at the top of a staircase, the woman that pressed up against him. She'd been accidentally pushed up against him, the bar getting crowded.

She was talking to him in a corner and then kissing him, a smoky sicky breath. 'I come from the remains of Sheffield,' he thought he heard her say. She hung on to him for a full five minutes, searching his chest and arms for something. He never knew, not until later, what she really looked like, it being dark and her hair around her, brushing all his face, and she was heavily made up so she looked very much like a doll, a desired effect.

Out in the warm night she led him across an open patch of land, she knew the way in the half darkness through dumps of rubbish and abandoned bicycles rusted and grown through with weeds. They followed the rise of the land, into its dips on a path that was trodden flat and shiny. The blocks of lights of houses to one side now, flats rising up around them.

She led them through the horde of dogs that seemed only interested in him, growling and snapping, and finally up the escape stairs to her flat, a badly worn carpet staring up at him. All around through the walls the movements and rumbles, the music, radio, television of other residents. He was sat there a while not knowing where she'd gone, but had to find the bathroom and was sick, and then he saw his face with its mud and scratches and sick now, his hair up in sticky tufts in the mirror and decided at least to wash, and use her toothpaste. After, wanting to leave some mark here, he scratched some paint off the back of the door, raising her heavy dressing gown hanging there to do so. Chips of paint under his nails, digging in.

Down a corridor with a chipped radiator leaking into a breakfast bowl he glimpsed a bedroom all dark, some thudding sound in there – were there people there? – eyes looking back at him, the light from the corridor only penetrating weakly. Some sort of mess, a blot beginning by the foot of the bed, but there was no smell. Besides the enveloping flat smell, something electric like her touch but dull also, a low thumping smell.

When he got back to the door of the room of what happened next he expected her to be gone, even though he could hear music starting up, some familiar chord arrangement from a song on the pub jukebox, but instead she was opening the flat door to some more men.

STAFF DEVELOPMENT

S ome mornings on the bus to work the dream of the house lingers and Jack expects to end up in the multi-roomed place, walking down corridors and staircases with his parents, both dead and resurrected and wife and daughter and granddaughter and dog and others he doesn't know, who all begin to jostle him with unsteady arms and falling-off fingers. It is like the manor house he visited last summer with Maggie. When he looks through the window though the glass turns to cellophane and he's inside the doll's house he built in the shed. It sits on a work bench. If he has to exit to avoid the scuffling, the grabbing for him, he'll have to drop – jump – to the chair, climb down a leg to reach the floor. Hope to hell the cat's not around.

Instead, every day, like today, Jack walks around the security barriers, nods to some, the whistler who doesn't stop whistling as he nods back, Ted Simms in his getting-shiny suit, and on into the vast building that looks all windows. On the stairs he coughs like a dog and Gregg coming up behind slaps his back. 'All right, Jack-o? See yer at break.'

Forgets his password again and he has to ring IT and they are, as ever, sarcastic. Tut tut, Mr Bond. And they're all of what – thirties at most? – following him, his every move, tracking him across the Atlantic or the other side of the world on the web he creates from his desk. His keyboard makes him spell the simplest words wrong. Worsd. Apicrot. Grils.

At desks around him people are urging their screens on, forward, 'Come on, then.' Someone is always applying cream or lotion to hands and neck. Today Patrick is showing off nicks caused by thorn or fence, evidence of a weekend walk. Jack tries not to look at Michelle's legs as she goes past. Doesn't succeed. This man, what's his name? – can Jack have forgotten? – pads up and down, looking, sniffing with a fine long nose, for anything wrong, flaws in the air and the concrete, the desks and the people.

A birthday card is waiting to be signed on his desk: Abigail warns him to hide it before Patrick, forty at the weekend, spots it. He signs it with no note, not like others who advise the man to get drunk or to buy a red sports car, or to hibernate until it's all over.

Jack realises he's been at this firm for almost the whole of Patrick's life. Married too, for much of it, and he wonders if Maggie is fed up, of course she is, all those years rolled up together. They'd gone fifteen years childless, visiting art galleries and stately homes (Jack more interested in the frames than the paintings, the fixtures than the history) instead of nurseries and parks. But then along came Gemma, out of nowhere it seemed, a little robust miracle, a fleshy piece of energy to wake them up.

Maggie's look when he met her would be called 'rock chick' now – T-shirt and jeans, long kinked hair, her dark eyes flashing through. Her eyes duller now, her face smudged with age like his, but still soft, not many wrinkles, still her teeth pushed forward her lips, the eternal pout, from then to now. The lives they've lived together from galleries and museums to sheds and kitchens, via the bedroom. Chuckle, tickle, shush. He titters and his colleague beside him lifts his head from coffee never knowing how to take this older man who talks to himself a bit, quietly, and maybe he's imagining it.

Jack focuses on work. All he has to do is attend to the emails that command, finish off the files from yesterday or yesteryear, chase up the missing orders hiding in a warehouse somewhere, acknowledge the report from the stationery subgroup. *With his comments.* He has no comments. It is simple, it is straightforward, it is staring him in the face, the C-drive full of folders. All he has to do is open them and get on.

*

Someone is always following Jack around second-guessing and peeping into his tilted world – he has a stoop now from somewhere, the age of him, the curl of death coming up from his toes already – measuring that corner of it, where wall met skirting met floor, is it all correct, is it all in balance, is it going to withstand the wind and rain? Everybody wants to know everything: how things were between them. Man and wife, cat and dog, tree and house on a scale of one to ten, what dances they'd attended, which sexual position they favoured and what was their favourite soap and what made Gemma, his only child born so late to them they'd given up, what made her up and marry that bloke, Gerard, that worthless bloke without an idea in his head or a penny in his purse? His purse. He has one. He stays home and lurks, he's done for her mentally, no violence at least, no sign, meandering on about socialism as if he knows what it is, that and computer games. He sucks the energy out of every room he's in with those dog-green eyes and shoulders down. It was drugs – *chasing the dragon*, he found out – watched a programme about it, the dragon was smoke from heated black dribble across silver foil. He found evidence by the shed in the mornings. It was no good talking to her: Gemma coming off the stuff was like a drunken doll version of herself, feet up on the rickety table he'd made, watching nothing on the box and her face blank. Spaced, she called it. Dad, I'm spaced. Static coming off her. But not any more, surely, with Jenny to look after. She's sensible that way. Takes after her mother, her straight-down-the-line mother. With Gerard though there's something more. Grudge somewhere. Full of bricks and rubble. Jack had seen him pumping some poor girl in an alley, an energy found for *that*, during some party he'd come out of, music following.

*

A woman comes down from upstairs. 'Follow-up session,' she says. She is wearing a pinky suit that makes Jack think of one of the figures – too small to be dolls, said Gemma at six – in the house. Stood for ever by the fireplace greeting visitors. Both had a lipstick smudge in the corners of their mouths. 'Then you'll be ready to cascade.'

Jack realizes after she has stood beside him smiling for a while, her eyes betraying no warmth and getting colder, as stones at night, that she wants him to get up, to offer his seat, like on the bus someone interrupting his daydream asking for tickets. He gets up and she sits down quickly as if in a planned, rehearsed manoeuvre, sighing a little at the strangeness of his mouse. 'It's back to front.' She clicks in her memory stick and opens the relevant program. 'I'm putting it on your desktop,' she says.

'How you get totals,' she says, 'how you get averages.' How to change screens and use other programs in conjunction. Jack says yes and I see and nods, and then when it comes to showing her what he has learnt, after they have swapped places again and he is to show her the totalling function, he tries to remember the movements of her fingers across the keyboard, he nudges a few keys and a figure turns up.

'Good, good,' she says but all he can remember now are the rings on her fingers, one gold but lacy, the red nails and the sound they made on the keys, the thin-linked silver watch, freckles on the back of her hands. The tops of her breasts, a white bra strap. The faint smell of soap around her. Imperial

Leather like Maggie at home, almost silent now and he doesn't quite know why.

*

They're there, checking, checking, cameras turning as he passes. Even the flowers bend as he walks by. Matt Helm. He's found somewhere though, a line crossed to safety, a space where they can't see, can't follow. Down beneath fire stairs, along a corridor no one uses, a room with a broken door lock that can be latched inside. He sits for half an hour or so a day amongst discarded items, clumpy computers and screens and cabinets and broken chairs, dust springing in his nose. Clutters of broken staplers and filing trays, wire and plastic.

Not like his masterpiece at home in the shed which he visits at weekends. Like smokers with their first cigarette he inhales deeply the smell of varnish, tool metal and sawdust as he enters the shed. He might inspect a chair, almost weightless in his palm, or pore over perspective drawings. Then he gets to work, measuring (with a metal ruler so worn the figures have almost disappeared), cutting, shaping and joining. After working for an hour or so, his muscles still buzzing from the motion of plane or saw, his teeth tasting where nails had been, he stops and gazes into each room, moving furniture about until it meets with his approval. He loves the way the panelled door opens with a little tug on its brass hinges. Inside it was the fireplace, window sills and skirting boards that cost him most effort. And the stairs – they turn corners and run to landings with Chinese fret handrails. He tries to keep to the period – mini chandeliers are suspended into the downstairs rooms, little bulbs that work – but Gemma wanted a telly for them to watch, the residents and visitors, the milkman with crate and unbent legs leant on the chaise longue. The TV screen now has a picture stuck on of Emma Peel, her eyes, nose and mouth, half smiling, for him.

These days you can get kits off the internet to put together the house he'd built by himself, working out the structure from books from the library which he never visits these days but keeps saying he will, and he will, maybe see the woman he brushed by in the aisles, her wave of black hair. Almost reached for it, that hair, changed his hand's direction to a shelf just in time.

He started it when Gemma was born; almost straight after he'd seen her slippery body emerge, to Maggie's final scream, anointed in oily colours. The smile that came and didn't leave for days. That night, when they finally chased him out of the ward, her newborn, bloody smell still all about him, he started on the plans, working out the measurements. And finished – never quite finished. There is always something to change: better-looking cutlery for the table; some new figures to see if they fit; a miniature Picasso, completely wrong era but what the hell, from his blue period – Maggie's favourite – to hang.

*

In the toilet washing his hands Gregg catches him and says straight away how so and so botched up a job and still got promoted. 'Doesn't that stink?' He leans in to Jack, can see a gold filling in a back tooth, feel the ginger breath on him. Gregg always knows, is keeping tabs: the downsizing, the rumours, the temporary staff they're going to bring in, who's fucking who.

'Always the same crowd. Round each other's houses for cheese and wine.' Gregg whines like a wolf, his head back. 'They all know too much, know where all the bodies are buried.' He turns, unzipping, to the urinal but carries on over his shoulder.

'That's the hold Ted Simms and Jackie Ripple have over them all. You know they're *liaising* don't you. Fucked in that stall there' – he nods to the side of him and Jack nods back at him in the mirror.

'Heard 'em, must have been a week ago, recognized his cough and her . . . little cry. Aahh, ah.' Gregg is pissing merrily now. 'I looked under the door but she'd pulled her feet up. Probably sat on his lap.' He zips up and turns. 'Fucking bastards. If I were you, Jack, I'd kick up hell the way they're treating you, you've been here longer than all of them put together. These warnings they're giving you are a disgrace.'

Jack has forgotten the warnings they've given him.

*

He could make it to his daughter's street and back in the lunch hour, just to say hello, spot how she's doing with Jenny, remember how wearing six-year-olds can be, but fun too. Talk about getting the doll's house ready for Jenny to play with, new things, a miniature computer maybe in the corner of a room, take out something, the bookcase because the books weren't real-looking, weren't separate things. Can't really bring it to her, would have to dismantle the shed to get it out. It wouldn't fit through door or window. Maggie was not surprised to hear of that. He would always cock something up. Look at the wonky table in their front room. He'd never been able to adapt his skills to their home, the larger scale defeated him. 'Can't you unglue, unscrew it, take it out in bits?' He couldn't bear the thought of that.

Jenny is the same age as Gemma when she was formally presented with it, a ribbon wrapped round, a bow tied between the chimneys. He continued to work on it though, from her sixth to her sixteenth, while she was there having little conversations between the characters, the figures he bought for her, an odd assortment, they tended to be firemen or police or film stars, Clint Eastwood in an eighteenth-century dining room demanding his beans on toast. Even in her teens, at fourteen, fifteen she'd come and move them about, a refuge from bullies, a gang who called her names and wrote *bitch* and worse about her on walls. He'd try and talk to her about them, the names called, the hurt, while sanding a door, or screwing in a hinge with a spectacle screwdriver, such close beady-eyed work, but she didn't want to say. Looking across to her though, her pinched face coming into focus, he thought she was glad of him there. Within arm's reach.

Then it was short skirts, boys, drugs. Those days of nothing doing, a tired insolence and then the pregnancy sprung on them all. The doll's house stopped then, unused, not played with, or upgraded or changed, while Gemma brought up

Jenny. She left for a starter home, one storey with a mezzanine, a balconied bedroom, and was still there with her non-starter husband. Gerard works on and off but never accumulates enough to leave. Maggie and Jack were together then, united in their help and time spent with Gemma, with Jenny shared between each other's arms. Baby sick back in their lives. Songs sung and stories told about wolves and pigs. Tolerating Gerard. 'Can't pin that bloke down,' Maggie would say after an hour of smiling at him. Sex returned, briefly, like a flare in the night. Before the cat reclaimed her lap.

And now, on visits, Jenny had found granddad's secret house in the shed, and tried all the doors and peered through the windows and got her big childish fingers into his rooms and the figures were once again moved about. He didn't mind, not even the inevitable breakages, a chandelier, a chair leg. He was there with her, sniggering over her fat teacher with her, asking about her dad, does he help her mum, does he read to her?

Jack drops in to buy a cake, a present for Gemma and Jenny, not for Gerard, Slim Jim, man about the sofa. He has forgotten supermarket etiquette, how you have to respond quickly to movement, shift with the queue or get a trolley in your thigh. And then there is the point where he thinks he doesn't have enough money and searches pockets he never knew he had, and the man behind tuts in smoker's throat until he finds the coins and counts them out and leaves carrying the cake out in front of him, can't have it on its side, its filling would come out.

Jack reaches the corner of her street and sees Gemma leave, go the other way, maybe he could shout but it's a long street, she's quite a way down so he tries to run with the cake box in front of him, but gives in and stops outside her house, he is almost looking down on its one boxy storey, seeing her disappear up ahead. Thin as her bloke with long black hair, always naturally curly, like her mother's all those years ago. He'd brushed it until sleek for years. She looks small now, pulled along by a little dog, smaller than when she was a kid. Dogshit everywhere on their strip of lawn below. He is taken over by the vision of her moments before – the turn from the door, the tug on the lead. Her knee turning in her dark jeans, away, that movement seconds before, takes over him. He stands still in the street, someone bringing out a black rubbish bag, a car reversing into a space beside him, outside her house with the cake box held before him. Halfway down a street curving to the left, blurred movement around him, like it is raining all around, at the edge of the space he creates. He can't move, he can't go on.

A woman wheels a pushchair past, the half-asleep baby wakes and points at him, a dog comes up and sniffs the back of his knees and he stands like a horse sometimes stands in a field, not moving an eyelid.

And then there he is, Gerard, the left-wing man, Jack and Maggie are on that side too, but he takes it too far. Shoot the royal family and cigar-smokers, redistribute wealth into his pockets. There was the night of the party when Jack caught him with another woman, he'd come out because he was drunk and needed air and made the mistake of walking a bit. His son-in-law's back, his uncovered arse going back and forth and the girl lifting her skirt up, sat on a wall. He knew the girl, friend of Gemma's, she was turning the other way with the thrusts but then her head turned round to see Jack. Later he'd said to Gerard, returning to the party, he'd waited for him, 'Why don't you piss off, run away with her?' And he'd never told Maggie, he didn't know why, he didn't want her to think about it. Or Gemma.

Here he is, not pissed off with anyone, not properly dressed, smelling of days indoors taking Gemma's and Jenny's and not his present from Jack's hands and talking into his face but Jack can't seem to respond to the cocked eyebrow and the shrugged shoulders of him turning away, except to say when he reaches the door down below him 'I s'pose she's out getting your drugs for you?' and he goes into the little house with the cake balanced on one hand.

*

He is late back; he goes down to his room again, under the stairs. It was on his third visit he masturbated. Sat on the wheeled chair, pushed up in a corner to stop it rolling. Thinking of the good days with his wife that fell upon them not at once, but after a struggle, misunderstandings. When she didn't get pregnant and they'd thought she never would, sex for a while became easy, slow and messy, but no rushing to clear up afterwards as before, an acceptance.

He also thinks, now, of Jackie Ripple, her flesh like ice cream to go with her name, leaving lipstick on him, all over him.

The sperm went, goes now, into the drawer of an old desk nearby, fingers clamped until he gets in the right position to let go, splash against the inside wood, whacking the dribble in. How nice to slide it shut after. The tissues he always carries, must be Maggie's training, now applied. The king of his room: anyone who came in would see a man exalted. As if his child had become rich and famous, safe. And happy, happier than any film star on a set. But also everything is pushed away, there is only him, having come, in a room beneath the stairs.

*

Jack is called into the boss's office, maybe he's been seen below, maybe someone's been in there and spotted something, a drawing he'd scribbled on wood, his pen dropped nearby. He passes the model under glass: a cleaner, whiter blanker building, figures outside, mini trees, a bus stop with a single-decker pulling away. The future.

There is a woman present who sits between them and looks from one to the other. His boss is telling him how appreciated he is, overall, but there are certain things, certain worries. Jack thinks he'll get on with everything now, he'll finish off those files, those training portfolios, he'll be an ace of the Supplies Department. An exemplar. How would it be if everyone came up and told him how good he was at his job and how loved by everyone he was? Didn't he know it, he was a *fixture*, been here from the start, when the company set up here, blimey been here pre-computers, he was the permanent figure in the house always doing the dishes.

His boss's moustache seems a little wonky and

Jack wants to ask if he's fucking Jackie Ripple in the gent's too much to concentrate on his appearance, or wouldn't that make you more meticulous with it, trimming the ends to point at her breasts while you're doing it. Gregg is convinced that Ted Boss is wearing a wig and Jack tries not to look to check at the hairline that does seem a little too neat, a little too perfect. No, she'd pull it off during all that activity and laugh, or maybe she didn't mind.

Everything he says, bewigged fucker of perfect wobbling flesh – just jealous – the man with notes in his hand, his *line manager*, begins with or contains 'just'.

'Just that you were seen running, stopping and then running again. Back the way you came.'

'We're just a little concerned now. Progress on your objectives has been slow, Erica tells me.'

'Well, we'll just see how it goes. No need for a big fuss just yet.'

Ted Shatmachine's eyes seem to have bits in them. Little red bits like bits of match-heads. The woman seems to be in a mist of grey air, when she speaks the grey air shudders as if plucked, although she doesn't speak much, she turns mainly to fucker – perhaps she wants a fuck too, perhaps they're all going off to the toilet together to have a merry threesome – and nods him on or slightly shakes her head or raises an eyebrow at what he is saying.

Jack is reminded of his forthcoming IPR, the goals he'd set in the last one, how far had he got? Were they achievable, did the training help? He has to break out of silo thinking. He hasn't completely blown it, he can tell from the smiles, the crease of his boss's mouth only seeming to one side because of the little scar on the other. Had he had a childhood accident? Is the window coming undone behind him? His boss moves back and forth in his chair, back and forth and Jack listens to the squeaks.

There is a fair chance everything will turn out just fine. Let's make this department the envy of the western world. Everybody with the correct supplies at the correct time. Not a pencil out of place. He just has to watch his footsteps, that's all, see where they go and stop them if need be. Was that clear? The square of the room was rounding out, beginning to spin, like someone has started to play some daft rock and roll like 'Rosalyn' by the Pretty Things, not the Bowie cover version.

All he has to do is watch where he's stepping, none of the dogshit in his daughter's house, none of that. Pass on his recent training. Let's see him back on track. That's the way, don't you see?

*

Gregg catches him on his way back to his desk. What were the ins and outs, what had Cocky Ted said now, should they get the unions in? We should just let them all have it, he machine-guns everyone coming down the corridor, ack-ack-ack, tell them everything we know, hey? He taps his nose at Jack.

He's only been at his terminal minutes when she arrives, it's not the same woman as this morning, she smells different: Sure deodorant, Jack reckons, tuna for lunch. Same hair as his daughter, except thicker, richer, cleaner like Gemma's was pre-Gerard days, fuller in figure too. Stood by the side of him as bright as strip-lighting talking.

More training, thinks Jack, when she mentions the program he'd been shown this morning, and he knows exactly where it is on the screen, it's on the desktop, he can go right there and double click it into life. Ping. 'There you are,' he says. 'Was there extra? Add-ons?' he'd heard someone say that recently.

She looks up and down the room, confused. Her stance, why is he noticing everyone's stance: his daughter in the street turning, Maggie standing by the door each morning to see him out, peck on the cheek, Gerard's head hung before him, get his nose into everything first, this girl as if about to flee and her lips pink with a gloss on them, he appreciates the gloss, her lips try to say something but decide not to. Then he realizes what her stance is trying to say, is telling him – he is supposed to train *her*. She is waiting to be trained, she is taking her first steps in office work, her career there maybe for ever like his, every day she'll come on the bus or drive or maybe she'll get out, she'll escape, she'll drop to the floor and fight off the bothersome cat, its claws and teeth, easily.

He gets off his chair again to offer it to her. While she settles and moves his strange mouse he goes to the window, hello hello Abigail and Patrick, I nod nod nod you and he tries to open the window beyond the suicide bar and whistles down at the security men sat in their little booth near where the bus drops him each morning, he thinks of Jesus in a hay barn, Hayley Mills and lemonade. He comes back to her, looking over her shoulder at him, along the burning pavements of his youth, the wasps and the bees, the land all blue.

How like his daughter she is, at one point in her life, how she might have been. How she could be loose-limbed and carefree, if she'd ditched Gerard, if she'd escaped. If she'd never met him. This new girl in his chair was Janette, she'd said, and gave him her hand, didn't she, didn't she have the cold quiet fingers reaching for him in the dream, on the bus, the ticket collector, the queue of zombies wanting more? Janette's eyes reflected all the sex she'd had and all the sex to come. Her eyes said he would be replaced, he would be gone soon. Like Gregg said, after over thirty years service. How the office would be without him, how it was already without him, once thought indispensable, everybody's pal, her eyes told him all this.

'What it does,' he says, eyeing the screen, 'is eat numbers. Nombres. Numbbums.' Janette nods, glad to talk about the program at last, after all the waiting. He leans over, so close to her hair and neck, to use the mouse and clicks on a figure in a box.

'It eats numbers,' Jack says, 'and has a big fat brelly.' He rubs his stomach like he is telling Gemma Red Riding Hood when she is old enough to be scared, to respond. 'Then spews them out, *regurgitates* them. We should serve them up, sever them up, on *little tiny* plates,' – he shows how big with the tips of finger and thumb – 'covered in roses to the royalty here, the bosses and ladies of the manor, don't you think?'

He says the hub, where they should go, to see the engine and wave at the driver, is downstairs. He'll take her there, would she care to stand up and follow him. He grasps her shoulder, it fits like a socket joint in his palm, he can feel her clavicle, her flesh and bra strap beneath white blouse, the warmth and shiver in it, the hardness of bone, her black hair nylon strands against the back of his fingers. He has it in mind they will both squeeze into that crowded small room he has made and he'll show her the furniture, the broken wheeled chair she could sit on and he'll bark out his orders like Clint Eastwood, only it will all be sexual.

ONE FOR THE ALBUM

She was among the crowd. Saw her sidelong, noticeable because of jeans amongst Marks & Spencer best, noticeable because she was like a trail of fire taking his eye round the room, through the dark knots of blokes he didn't know, standing foursquare and thinking of getting drunk, the stages of it, and maybe of her body as she moved on and through women who pecked at her shoulders with bags and hands and she stayed there a while, stepping out onto the dance-floor occasionally to fill her body with the blasting music. Then she settled with her crowd, other women her age, sat and the smile dropped off her face as she sipped a drink, as she watched the others around her.

That was it then, and he was bored with the friends who had brought him here, to this do.

Who had engagement parties these days? He looked at the girl showing the ring – pleasant smile, rather a mean slope along the cheekbone – seeing her circulate around the edge, and he wondered at the formality of it. It was another weekend gone and just drink and stories of other times to remember of it. Talking now of cars and football, the mouths of his fellows puckering at the sounds of things, carburettors and Wright-Phillips, and picking on some other girl, some obvious blonde dancing to choose, to remark on. Blonde and her boyfriend the types to get up on the floor and never get off, just to piss or refill, to rest a moment and laugh at each other. His eyes were further back.

He made his slow way away into people he didn't know, listened to their conversation, about the last do where there was a ruck in the car park, where there was someone collapsed in the toilet. From one group to another from hope to joke to banter and pushing, via toilets where it was too early yet for a collapse, for spew, back round a corner he dipped to get a better view, her radiance dimming as he got to the edge of her group. Sat nearby to take in more the style of her crossed legs, one palm on her thigh, a finger reaching her knee and got up at the same time as her, her wide hips in jeans and the legs not straight turning by his, touching. Larger and fuller than the bride-to-be but something of the same slant in the face, a distant relation. She was like a real thing next to him.

'Going for a fag?' he guessed.

*

'Social pariahs,' he said to her, looking out over the cars, moths around a light above his head. 'They'll be banning it altogether soon.'

'It's on the cards,' she said, her teeth large and uneven. She asked how he got here. Turned out she *was* a second cousin, visiting others for the weekend and dragged along like him. She looked at her cigarette and then at him, her eyes steady into his. 'See you next fag break, then.'

He followed her back into the noise and warmth, her long form seemed to twist in and out of the crowds so he lost sight. Then someone stopped her, and he could see more. He watched her smile and reply. Her nose was not upturned or downturned but full-on looked a little pinched. She stood as if she was leaning on something, her hands behind her back. Someone else came up and he watched her turn again, the little half-turns then from one to the other, her head inclined.

He went to lean against the bar and have a quick whisky from where he watched her more in the middle of the room while others met before him, exchanging greetings, kisses and lifelong promises. The engaged girl came close enough to smell her perfume, and now looked to him really thrilled, in the centre of so much laughing and teasing, looked as if she felt the world opening up for her. Behind her the blonde and her sweating boyfriend danced on.

He wondered how long to wait before re-signalling her with two fingers at his lips, inhaling imaginary smoke, but it was her that came up behind him, leaning close to his ear to feel her fag and drink breath, 'Got some weed in the car – fancy it?'

*

'Let's drive,' she said when they got into the car, chucking a tobacco tin at him. 'You roll.'

He rolled, not a very good one with the motion of the car. The city began to light up as they got close to its centre and they glided under its heart along the groove of an underpass, the arches going by exhaust-stained. Then they emerged upwards and kept going, shooting in an arc over another congested junction, then rows of lights span out and up around them. He took long, deep draws on the joint before passing it to her.

He assumed they were looking for a suitable place to stop – since neither of them lived here they'd have to find somewhere secluded and do it in the car. A park, an empty factory car park surrounded by a tall fence. Maybe just a lay-by. But he realized as they went on, as they came out of the city on a lit motorway, that she had somewhere else in mind. He watched the road, there was little traffic, then her in the passing lights, the long hair, the flame that signalled him, tucked behind large ears. She was quiet, contained. Thinking. Forehead shaping lines now and then and then smoothing out. One-word answers: 'Thanks,' 'No.' He tried to place her: the dope, the jeans, the tape collection he started rummaging through at her request.

'Tapes?' he asked.

'Not my stuff, I borrowed the car,' she said. 'Anything will do.' So he pressed the play button, it was Radiohead and he turned it down.

The motorway ended, became dual carriageway and they swept through almost deserted towns and villages, the odd drunk pissing against a fence or stumbling out in the road. Once they passed an accident at a junction – two cars, one crumpled, and yellow-jacketed policemen and ambulance men crawling over it. One waved them around the messy scene.

Just as they'd silently agreed not to talk or ask about the people behind the rings on their fingers, even though at almost every juncture, at least to begin with, he wanted to, or found it hard to purge his sentences – 'We were on holiday once . . .', 'We had an accident like that . . .' – he knew he couldn't ask about the destination.

Then the first mountain presented itself. We're in fucking Wales, he thought. He'd never been to Wales. She drove expertly as the roads she took narrowed and angled upwards. Side-on her face was a dance of light and dark dots, colour only in her lips. He watched as she manoeuvred around double bends, up steep gradients, watched her arms and legs change gear, slow or speed up. 'You're a good driver.' 'Well it's hardly Monte Carlo,' she said.

They dipped down to a curve that seemed to take them over a lake. A slight mist, droplets on the windscreen obscured his vision but the lake seemed to go on for ever, like a sea. They pulled up shortly after in a lay-by under some trees. She said she had two wraps of whiz too. It wasn't something he did normally; sure, he said. The lake outside might have been a reservoir. She'd been here before; maybe come with some other bloke, he thought, a Welsh bloke brought her here.

Their hands went to each other without much kissing. She used her hand and mouth on him until he was rigid, and still working him softly with one hand she retrieved her mobile from her bag and took a picture. For a moment his erection and lap were lit up.

'One for the album,' she said in the sudden dark.

'How do I fare?' he asked, coming round from the flash.

'Don't know yet,' she said, moving closer.

*

The going was easy at first along the edge of the water, the water shimmering under drizzle, the drops of water falling between them in half-light, some light reflected from somewhere across the sky, her hand extended backwards to help him over the pocked, curling land, a line of view opening out to a poorly lit valley, and then the valley got thin and angled. No houses, just jutting woods, and a view fizzling out, darkening, lightening, mist and dark, and she tugged him on past a boulder, circling a stand of woods and on through stone coming up close to his shoulder, he felt the stone clot above him. Already the touch of her, breast and bone, was leaving his fingers, but his mouth was still clogged with her various tastes.

She said she was looking for a cave, and they gathered wood as dry as possible on the way up. 'Ug, ug,' he said. 'You marzipan, me plain,' she said and beat her chest. He realized it wasn't a Welsh boyfriend who had brought her here, but her family; she'd been a kid here. On holiday maybe, this cave her den. When she found it she whooped and searched around it but whatever she was looking for wasn't there. Maybe she'd scratched a message on the wall that time had erased.

She got a fire started and they huddled together in its paltry smoke, tried to look down to the lapping water below, saw mountains loom across from them, detail after detail, scree tumbling with rocks, a white line of water fell, twisting on its way down, sheep bobbling the grass, up to their knees in mist. Individual trees became distinct from the mass, and they watched the sun come up with a shared joint like a couple of hippies at a festival. Again he found it difficult not to mention his history, to keep things out of his speech. He had the feeling that for her this childhood place was not what she'd expected, what she'd wanted, but she was making the best of it.

He looked at her as much as he could, light showing up her lined but young features, the small nose almost lost. He thought of all the big-faced women in his life, the ones, like her, who hold their face back and a little to one side, a rather affected look in reality, a little haughty he supposed, but there it was, maybe he liked the hint of ice they gave, maybe he didn't altogether want warmth. They didn't fuck again.

He didn't want to go in the morning. She said she'd go without him. Leave him stranded on the mountain and maybe snow on the way. The weather can change, she said, and already purplish clouds were massing. The car was about half a mile away, a small red patch visible through the trees below.

At last they rose from the damp ground, and ran down, sliding, holding on to rocks and trees to slow their descent. He fell onto mud and she helped him up, laughed at his trousers flapping wetly, the city shoes curled with damp. Along the lake they walked arm in arm like a normal couple out for a stroll until they reached the car, and she said roll another one for the journey.

*

'You've got your picture,' he said, his mouth dry from the whiz, from the night. The sixty-mile journey back was telling on him, the city that neither of them knew well coming into view. He was scratched, stank of fire, wood, mud and her. 'Can I just know your name? Something for something.'

'Rose,' she said, but she hesitated too long. He knew she was lying.

THE DITCH

In my future I die slowly – chewed like gristle in the office teeth, spat out twisted to fend for myself. I won't be a successful tramp with a collection of trinkets and a song for myself, more a whining homeless like the one in town here, cadging pound notes for drinks. My body will play me up – wrench me round as if something behind bothers. I'll sleep in bushes and ditches and bus shelters and empty houses and barns across the countryside.

During *Macbeth* the teacher's foreshortened arm points me out: 'Marshall's a cynic already,' using me as a visual aid. Cream-faced loon.

'Tomorrow and tomorrow and tomorrer,' Dunne the grunt intones, looking for a laugh at the end, stood, his shirt out over his lumps. The teacher's fingers douse an imaginary flame at the brief candle bit. The question for homework: Did Macbeth hate Banquo or were his feelings more subtle than that?

At lunchtime I sit near a rain-washed window reading. I'm not always alone, five cowards cowering are better than one – they might not get round to you. I've lost count of the toe stampings, dead legs, hair yanks and spit-ats I receive daily, from Sid (named after Sid Vicious) and his gang. I look at my ugliness in the reflection, the book on my lap and think *I'd* bully me.

In the last lesson Spike the Christian history teacher makes some remark about me being in reverse gear as I try to remember my future. Grass and stone calls. He wants me to debate 'Can God Save Us?' having proved last week – so he thinks – that He exists, against my argument to the contrary. He wants to crush with moral logic, and enliven his lesson. He wants my help to stop the lads exhausted from playing rugby and bullying from falling asleep, but I fail to oblige.

I get on the bus home, making my way through the bellows and pushes and stomping of the teenage herd, squirm to my usual halfway-down seat, next to nerd number 2. His crime was as much his refusal – his running out of the lab – to cut up the cold eyes of cows and examine and smell the vitreous liquid and the soapy lens, as his yet undescended testicles and sparse pubic hair, evident in the changing rooms. I watch the half-busy town go by over his lap. Those around moon at the girls' school emptying or whistle through the little slide-back windows at the top, angling their heads. I watch them too, groups of grey skirts and blue tops, unbuttoned, heads bent to each other, watch their numbers thin out as we drive by, the boys comparing the breasts and knees of the ones they've seen. Then Sid with his biroed swastika on his neck turns his attention to me and signals to his cronies. Their hands slide towards me, from over and around the seat, and mock-choke me, and I splutter as they sing a song they've made up about me. Something about shitting in shit bags – sung to a teabag advert theme – and eating it the next day. They crowd around and prod and scream and I look at the chewing-gummed and fag-end floor and try not to listen to the pulsing choruses, louder and louder, of 'Ooh-ooh Martian'.

The last outing we had, I followed the others round the museum. Did I hate them all – the ones in front who spat and giggled and slyly punched, the teacher a child's version of an adult, crumbling like crayon marks before them – or were my feelings more subtle than that?

Out of the town and through lanes dropping off the odd (very odd) farmer's boy on the way and finally through the two lines of coppice halfway up the short hill. Beyond there's my estate, cubes stuck in the countryside, tacked on to the small-church, one-pub village. The vicar with his hair like grey grass round a boulder is counselling a fat woman with a pram by the bins outside the strip of four shops necessary for life: mini-supermarket with offie, post office and a new video section; hairdressers; fish-and-chip shop; Chinese takeaway. A dog tied to one scratched green bin starts to bark and sets off the baby as I sneak down long-grassed alleys to my back door.

I have my dealings with my family, retrieve biscuit and milky coffee, and retire to a corner amid the babble. Jules, my seventeen-year-old sister, dandles her big-headed baby, permanently surprised at what he's been brought into. Her husband-to-be also lives here but is not home yet from the metal-seal factory that dominates the area beyond a further shielding coppice and stream behind our house, and often he's late, laden with beer and smelling of it underneath the suds and oil and with the dust of metal filings on his clothes. My older brother, Dom, sits around like a throwback to the sixties, out of work, strumming on his hand-lettered twelve-string guitar and getting in the way.

Dinner is gunky with sludgy spuds and sprouts catching in my throat. As Mum collects plates at the end with great concentration like some kind of juggler, my stomach lurches. I choke inside, the food seems to clog all my sensory systems so the room bobs and blurs. Or blobs and burrs. I stare at the tablecloth, grip on, scratching the wood underneath. A voice says stop, stop now please, gently but insistently, stop now please. This happens occasionally; I follow my usual strategy, concentrate, strain, shut my eyes. A flash of trampdom – the unbelted, ripped trousers, my nose always clogged, my eyes slits against the weather. I blink it away and I'm calm and can look at them again: sister, brother, mother. In my father's place, the laughter of crowds.

Later I compose sugary farts to accompany strummer-boy, humming rather than singing apart from the odd phrase, Beatles or Kinks stuff.

Eight o'clock and all's the same. Mum comes in flapping, says I used to find homework a pleasure, asks about my PE kit for tomorrow and about my weekend job – was I ready? Why don't I see more of Terrence these days, and when am I going to tidy up my room properly? – until I leave for said room. I put on the tape player she bought me last year – 'to celebrate becoming a teenager', giving me a kiss she hasn't repeated, on the forehead. To please her I play rock or punk loudly now and then, pretend to dance in front of the mirror, though I really like soul, Aretha Franklin. 'People Get Ready'; 'Respect'.

At the weekend I'll go and earn my tenner working for the Gloucester-accented North brothers with their tins of baccy, checked shirts, gap-toothed smiles and crude attitudes. They are contracted workers providing services for the metal-seals factory – everything done on a wink, cash in hand, at lunchtime pub meetings. You have to follow them around for an hour before they'll pay you. I move furniture in the empty offices, or remove rubbish from around the grounds. My first job was digging ditches to lay pipes but I proved too weak, now I fetch and carry and help out. Sometimes I go into the factory proper, still part-busy with Saturday overtime, and remember when my dad brought me here to see where he worked. I look over to that corner where metal slides out of the furnace evenly over rollers and men in masks manoeuvre the molten flow with remote controls.

I resist family outings, car rides where I sit in the back and am jolted by Dom who approaches corners like life, sloppily, in order to eat sandwiches in front of tatty enclosures of roaming cassowaries, or else round the laden tables of uncles and aunts with cousins pushed at me as if they're the answer to all my problems, all my questions about existence, and stay in by myself, wandering the seven rooms of my life so far. How I'll miss these dry comforts later when I lie in some sharp and mossy place, feeling the stones as I sink into mud and grass. Always, everywhere in this house, the absence of my father.

I always visit their room, the room in which I suppose I was conceived – the three of us were at two-year intervals – which is now frilled and patterned and draped but was it then, when he was here, the almost mythical time for me? The odd photo of him and his grin and half-cocked nose, always looking out beyond the photo. The photo shows different wallpaper, different objects on the sideboard beside him. The miniature Eiffel Tower is now replaced by a chalky dog, nose up like his. When he was here, I remember, twice a month, more or less, he'd slap me – not that hard – on the top of my head, and then draw me to him and say sorry. His hugs were warm, awkward, sweaty. In the wardrobe, shoes warped by his outsized big toes still line up and the suit he left hanging smells of him, the underarm lining. It's too small for my beer-driven bloated brother, but maybe OK for me in a year or two.

In their room I sit on the bed, my eyes getting used to the gloom. Through the window I can see chimneys and aerials across the road, and beyond, hills, and above, the vast night breathing. Black-dot birds dip and swirl. Behind me, I imagine, a lover reclines, or sits half out of bed watching my back. We're in our twenties, a space before I fall. She holds the white sheet against her bosom, the room's yellow and white: colours too bright, like an advert, but she is there, warm blonde flesh, flickering in my future too. I blink and it's grey and I'm in the muddle of mother's bedroom, her dull sleep smell adding to the damp already folded into the air.

A girl I met once at a rare party kept feeding me sweets. She had those little coloured bands round one wrist that marked her as retro, a hippy, and had come with a group of them, yellows, flowers, headbands, loons swishing the floor amongst all the black-clad punks. I sat in the kitchen of the parent-free house swigging cider as nonchalantly as I could. She came and stood close, her small bra-less breasts outlined through her tie-dyed T-shirt. Her black hair was half tied back, leaving a swathe hanging. Her mates had commandeered the music and Hawkwind was playing. Her navel swayed between bony hips but after she stuffed me with liquorice allsorts (she didn't mind me licking her darkening fingers), she moved on, pleased with herself, gave me the peace sign as she left, and joined her little colourful group to jump around and further show off her litheness, twisting from one to the other.

Now in my room I look out as our fat-arsed neighbour waddles in the dull but starred evening to collect garden implements. In the garden the worms turn. Beyond, the sound of playing kids dismantles the air. There was a hollow tree; kids young enough to crawl up into its fibrous darkness choked it in summer. I was one, once, before some of them set fire to it and you came out drawn on with charcoal, smudged across your face and shirt.

What do I live on in the final days? Fillet of snake, no doubt, and sheep's eyeballs. I put some music on, allow the woman's voice precedence until it is alone in the room. At last I am a wisp, a stray light fallen on this chair.

I gradually feel the grass and nettles grow through me, the earth in my mouth, a landscape of nests and escapes and tunnels for worms and insects and small birds. The ditch over time claims me, my eyes two pebbles dully counting stars while I turn into a boned, grassy mound, a healing, an interruption to the ditch.

HUDDERSFIELD VERSUS CREWE

'Pools? God. Yes. Years since I did those. Frank never bothered. It's a man's thing isn't it, the pools? The lottery's more women.'

I reassured her – lots of women on my round. Single women, too. She gave me a sharp look at this.

'I wouldn't know where to start with filling it in.'

I could help her. I wouldn't mind showing her.

'I'm just going out.' She was dressed up, plenty of eye make-up, a necklace catching street light. A long, long neck. 'Call next week, could you? I'm Kath, and you?'

'David. Dave.'

How things start. I nearly didn't call. I was drumming up business on a second round I'd just taken over. I wasn't having much luck among the narrow rows of terraces whose sloping streets always seemed to be in fog that autumn and winter. It was the last house I tried before I trudged back under the motorway home.

*

I've always kept up the pools round, all through the other jobs I've had, mainly factory work, but also shop assistant, maintenance man in a block of offices, supply postman. Itty-bitty jobs, my wife Barbara called them. But that's not quite right – the maintenance job lasted six years until the firm relocated to Scotland. The pools always brought in that little bit extra. It also got me out of the house.

The way I saw it, towards the end, that's what they wanted – me out the house. It seemed to me they were ganging up on me. My wife would say 'You're just short of useless' ('just' being the money I brought in – she often earned more with her part-time nursing). 'Why do you bother pretending to take an interest? You're so full of yourself,' she'd continue. 'Apologies for breathing,' I'd say.

My daughter Ruth was no better. When I talked to her there was this sneer on her face the whole time. As if she couldn't quite believe what she was seeing. If she could she'd lie in front of MTV all day. An essay she wrote, on 'My Dad': 'He shaves in the sink and Mum is sick of him.' I pointed it out to Barbara. She said, 'And?'

The cat was held in more esteem. I'd come home weighed down with shopping and park the stuff in fridge and cupboard, the kid's chocs, her yoghurts, my beers, and not say a word to either of them, busy anyway with TV-watching, hoovering, on the phone. Of an evening we'd shuffle past each other between fridge and sofa. There didn't seem much to look forward to; I was sitting on the toilet reading pension leaflets and working out sums. My hair getting wirier, more like a wig each day. My latest job didn't help – forklift driving in a warehouse – and a lot of it was waiting about between deliveries. I looked at the days in my life and could see no difference in them, unless we won the pools. I'm sure Barbara thought that as a poolsman I should have been able to arrange that.

*

The night I first went into her house I smoked so much I silently vowed to smoke no more. 'Blimey. No doubt you can keep up, then?' She wanted me to catch the doubleness of her words.

We sat on adjoining sofas in this small room. The former tenant's heavily patterned wallpaper

– she hadn't bothered to decorate though she'd been there three years – made it seem even smaller. We pored over the coupon I'd put on the coffee table, our hands and knees close. Her hair smelt of tea, it was the colour nicotine leaves on the fingers. I explained the green panel, the blue panel, the booster entry. I could see how her eyes smiled – not quite her mouth – at that. She thought the crosses were like marks on a treasure map.

Every week she found some excuse for inviting me in. *EastEnders* on the television while she searched her bag for change. She always asked advice. 'Shall I go for Huddersfield versus Crewe? Sounds like a draw to me.' I told her to stick to the same numbers, the same pattern. 'It's the best way.' She wouldn't. She'd come to the door and say she was on the phone and to come in and I'd watch her squat in a position she must have assumed hundreds of times, she looked so comfortable. All the time I looked over the planes and corners and curves of her face for the beauty I saw there.

Sex with her was like dishes being served, one after the other, and all tasting new, ingredients you recognized but a new mix. She quite liked me to eat off her. I spent a long time gazing at her pale, rounded, marked skin, like a hoard of gold in the light from the anglepoise. It was a lazy, dabbling kind of sex, but occasionally she clung and dug into me hard, kneading, as if to make something new of my flesh. Afterwards I was tingling, felt the blood reach right down to my fingers and toes.

By now I was always late in from the round and told Barbara I always would be – meeting a mate down the pub. She took this with a shrug – 'Enjoy yourself.'

Thoughts of Kath cut through the week, far-off lights calling through the fog as I stomped around the house. 'Wotcher, strop-features,' said Ruth. 'Villa losing, are they?'

Barbara finally noticed. I was spending too long in the bathroom looking into the mirror trying to figure out what it was Kath saw in me. 'You got a woman?' Her dark eyebrows arrowed. 'Yeh – you,' I said, but soon after I left, Kath had been saying I could, I should, and moved three quarters of a mile away under the always-roaring motorway to the other side.

*

We'd eat cheese on toast and do little. Didn't go out much. It was a relief to come home to such quiet. She liked me for the oil on me, the way I talked, apparently. My steadiness. I was 'handsome, in a way'. 'What way?' 'A way I like.' I liked her for the difference she presented. She was a Brummie but had spent time away and lost – almost – the accent. She was so pale after Barbara's dark looks. 'My ghost,' I called her.

'You can save me from going under in this place,' she said, nodding towards the window. The fog was a mixture of weather and fumes from the battery factory, she said. She said she could hardly breathe out there and nothing would grow in the garden, a short one backing on to the motorway embankment. (She was later disappointed to find I didn't have the green fingers she wanted, but I made up for it in other ways.) She said the neighbours stole her catalogue parcels. She talked of moving out, somewhere 'nice' – Sutton, for example, but we couldn't afford that.

I didn't think it was so bad. True, when the motorway cut our district in two when I was a kid it was deemed the rougher part. Barbara in particular didn't want Ruth mixing with the boys from here. But on my round I found little difference in the people – some were friendly, I got a kiss and a tenner from someone who won a couple of thou third dividend, others guarded their property as if you had a second job as a burglar. I had to admit it wasn't as pleasant with the high sagging factory walls, the shunting yards and the huge weathered billboard (a fading 'It Could Be You') welcoming you, but then the other side wasn't exactly Solihull either.

*

Kath was an actress. 'An actor,' she'd say, 'an actor.
I am an actor. Or at least I was.' We watched the
videos that proved it. In one she opened the door
to police, in curlers, a shrugged-on dressing gown,
and was pushed aside. An ageing moll. (I got her
to play that role later, and I was a policeman who
stayed to interrogate her.) A speaking part in
the cable company ad. No, she couldn't tell the
difference between a BT phone and this one. Except
when the bills came in. Behind her was Central
Library and the glugging fountain in Chamberlain
Square. I saw that a few times, and noted again
how she was cast as ordinary, hair blowing in
the wind looked almost grey, and yet she seemed
young to me. She actually got her phone installed
and bills paid for a month as part of the deal. 'I
made so many calls I ran out of people to call. My
daughter got sick of me.'

Her daughter, Bernadette – Bernie – was going
to be the one that did it. Actually be an actor. She
was tall, brilliant, her face so expressive, camera-
friendly. I asked her how she knew since she hardly
saw her now. Bernie, at fifteen, had decided to live
with her father after the divorce, and took his side
always. 'All right, it's true at that time I was a bit
messed up. I was seeing Frank who I later moved

in with, and doing drugs, a bit.' She regretted not fighting for custody through the courts. That would have sobered her up and Bernie would have seen her how she could be: straight, responsible. Like now. On top of things. Bernie would have stayed and by now Kath would be visiting her in London, seeing her perform. Standing by her in photographs.

Kath told me it was her who'd done all the work with the baby and her bringing up. It was her who'd made Bernie what she was. How could she choose the father who'd left her to her own devices all those years? Neither was he the saint he made himself out to be. I sat and agreed with her word for word, because I felt too how children can be so heartless, unthinking.

*

One night in spring I came in from the job and she was listening to Virgin Classic Album Tracks – U2's 'She Moves in Mysterious Ways'. Doing a little dance. Sunlight was squeezing in from the tiny shred of sky visible above the embankment.

'Do you think I'm mysterious?'

'Yes, very.'

'I used to think I was an alien. Or been abducted by aliens. But maybe I just dreamt it and you know some dreams are so real they become real.'

Again I looked over the paleness of her face, the tiny red marks – neck creases – under her ear, her hair tied back gold in the late slanting sun. I wanted to get to the bottom of her.

'So you're an alien. I always wondered. Your slippery skin. Your bug eyes.'

'No, I mean it. I mean, I'm not me.'

'Possessed, maybe.'

The whole room was gold and she golden in it. I moved towards her.

*

She told me how handsome Frank was: 'All he had was nice black hair and a good couple of eyes. When all's said and done it's the eyes that get me on a man every time.' And how she missed her ex – a steady type like me, and although it brought a bad taste to my mouth, I understood it, it was a kind of accounting for herself. And because a similar thing was happening to me – thoughts of my wife, soon to be my ex, had begun where for long years when she was right beside me I'd done nothing but try and block her out.

Little things – finding Barbara's photo-booth picture, the one that didn't make it into the passport fifteen years ago, in the inside pocket of a jacket I'd hardly worn and picked up on a forage back at the house. When Kath played music it was seventies stuff – T. Rex and Roxy Music. Her favourite single was Hawkwind's 'Silver Machine'. Barbara had similar tastes, only Kath liked the treble high and Babs liked it low, more bass.

I thought it was to be expected really and it needn't be a problem, but one night during my first summer at Kath's I lay awake watching her undress. To cool us we had the window open behind drawn curtains. Her skin was still pale but glowed from the warmth of the day. I recalled a scene from an early holiday with Barbara. Lanzarote in June. She took off her bikini in the hotel room. The evening light and her deep tan made it look as if she'd put on some bizarre skin-tight costume that left her private parts exposed. Through the night with Kath snuggling close but not wanting sex, I seemed to hear the sea breaking outside the window – maybe the noise of the motorway.

*

No one seemed to call on Kath; the phone never rang. The people on my round didn't know much about her, though they remembered Frank. I asked her where she'd been going the night I first called, all dressed up. She said some function, she couldn't remember, as if she went to them all the time.

One night though when I got in, still thinking it strange to get my key ready on the corner of this street dominated by the motorway that rose above it, she was on the phone. She was crying, the receiver in her lap. Bernie was on the other end. I took the phone from her, despite her protests.

'Can't you be nice to your mother for once?'

'Who are you?' said the voice. 'Where's Frank?'

'Frank's gone. I'm here now.'

'But who the fuck *are* you?' And she put the phone down.

After that was our first argument. Because she hadn't told her daughter about me. How was that going to make me feel? I said she should write to her, explaining I wasn't some fly-by-night. But she was still wet-faced from the call and I stopped and put my arms wide. 'You've got to believe in me. We've got to stick together.' She agreed and came close and kissed and promised everything would be all right. There was nothing wrong.

*

I was still doing my old round. Which is how I found out my wife was no longer there, nowhere in the district. A former neighbour said something about her going. Sure enough I called on our old house, even though Barbara had cancelled the pools when I left, and a tall Asian in white robes and waistcoat opened the door. I asked him did he want to do the pools but he wanted to get rid of me and didn't give me a chance to look through, past him, to my old world.

I didn't go back. I gave up my round there. I knew she'd have to contact me soon, for the divorce to progress. She did and she said she didn't require maintenance any more, they were all doing quite nicely now.

In her letter, which was almost friendly, she said I should keep in contact with Ruth, and that I should want to, and I did, although at one time I hadn't, of course. Ruth came to our house a couple of times, nodded disdainfully at Kath and sat and watched television until it was time for me to take her back. So instead I met her on my own, once a month, and we'd go out, to the cinema mainly, the latest blockbuster – she liked special effects, *Independence Day*, *Total Recall*, and so did I – and a McDonald's after. More recently she wanted to go for a meal, she introduced me to Greek food, or a new balti at some place across the city. For many years, I told her, our diet had had to be as bland as possible because otherwise she wouldn't eat it. She said she was grown up now – she'd be sixteen soon.

She tells me of her new life, how Babs has changed – brighter, more relaxed, apparently, from the burden of me being lifted – and of Robert, her stepfather. I was glad to hear her say that though he was 'all right' and worked hard he was a bit of a creep. But then anyone over twenty-five was a bit of a creep to Ruth.

She pointed out that what I was doing, had done, was nothing new. Just the same as thousands of others, like her friends' parents, middle-aged prats running after younger women. But she's not, I said, only a few years. Same as your mother. (I turned it into a compliment for Kath when I got back but she didn't want to hear anything Ruth might have to say.) Anyway, I added, your mother's no angel. I was referring to a brief (I think) affair she'd had years before which Ruth wouldn't have known about but she nodded as if she did.

*

We – Kath and me – went to see *The English Patient*. I practically had to force her out of the house. I thought she'd want to go. 'You're the actress,' I said. She didn't correct me. Before she went she read up on the film and during the screening she told me the critic's opinions.

After we dropped into a nearby bar, across from the Hippodrome. I thought she'd like to be near a theatre. When we'd settled in a corner by the window I asked her if she couldn't refrain from telling me what everyone else thought of the film during it, so I could make up my own mind.

'Oh,' she said, sniffing, and looked out at the crowds leaving the theatre. It was nice to be out amongst people. I'd thought about going back to the Villa again. I knew Kath wouldn't want to come, but she wouldn't mind me going.

'No, I don't mean I don't want to hear, but after the film.'

'No, you're perfectly right,' she said, still looking away. I gazed back towards the bar. I had been sat in a corner like this once out with Barbara. She was at the bar and I watched as a few men glanced across at her, some not so slyly. How she stood on her toes in strappy shoes, waiting to be served, then dropped back on her heels. The backs of her knees bent in, one a deeper hollow. How she moved steadily across the room holding the two pints and not spilling a drop underneath her narrow, lopsided smile. A man was singing as we came out and for once it was a good, strong voice. A small mob that had been shouting and chucking things stopped to listen. His voice became larger, only drowned out by a passing bus, and he got on his knees for the finale. Me and Babs clapped and whistled for the man in the padded sleeveless anorak with his arms wide.

Me and Kath got the bus back to the motorway intersection and stopped on the corner by the billboard to light cigarettes. She had been quiet on the way home despite the rowdy passengers trying to get everyone to sing 'Three Lions'. She turned; she was smiling, she was trying hard. 'I'll get a job. Do something useful with myself, you see.' 'That's great,' I said, and apologized for what I'd said in the bar. For some reason we didn't carry on down the street, but stayed until we'd finished smoking. We watched lights arc into the sky as cars went up slip roads. Then we put our arms round each other and hugged for what we'd done in this life, and what also we had no control over.

*

She did get a job – at the local supermarket on the one till. But she didn't like the customers, got flustered with special offers and always feared armed robbery. She came home jittery. She took more and more time off and in the end I told her she should leave the job if it was getting her down so much, we could cope. (I thought she'd get the sack soon anyway.) But then we'd definitely have to stay here. She didn't care, she was grateful I'd said the words, and she rang up, went to get her wages and never went there again.

She hardly ever went anywhere again. One Sunday afternoon with fog again at the window she cried at *Oliver!* the musical, as much at Bill Sykes and Nancy's twisted relationship as over Oliver's plight. During the film I'd laughed at the mock-cockney and now wished I hadn't. I'd say that was the beginning.

She started spending days in bed, or wandered downstairs in her dressing gown (I said was she auditioning for her old role but she didn't seem to know what I was talking about). I'd say, 'What you been up to?' 'Not a lot,' she'd say. She always had excuses – 'If I'd gone out I'd have *drownded*.' (Mimicking my accent.)

She got a cat, I don't know where from. It didn't like me; it scratched me. 'It's only a kitten,' she said. It wasn't. She put a dirt tray in the kitchen. 'You have to train it to go outside,' I said. She wouldn't. Her fingers started smelling of cat food. Her breath was fags, but then so was mine.

At night with Kath in bed I zapped through cable channels as Kath did in the day and evening – 'Where's the zapper?' she said once. 'Things are no good without the zapper.' I watched the weather in Norwegian, *Exotica Erotica*, Tommy Vance and MTV, which I imagined Ruth would be watching. You had to hand it to Barbara, she had turned out much better than I would have imagined – I looked forward to seeing her now. I thought of her early life, not so much babyhood because that was just a whirl of broken nights, mopping up, feeding, bathing. But of later when she grew into who she was. How she couldn't get enough of learning. The phases she went through – I remember her doing the Ancient Civilizations, copying the alphabets of the Egyptians and Phoenicians (the trouble she had with that word) and writing messages in hieroglyphics. She made her bedroom into a museum, with a sign on the door and exhibits (bits of broken plates, paintings she'd done), and charged admission. Her Bugs Bunny teeth, her shining face, the freckles beginning that she would hate later. The singing of hymns, trying to do handstands in the kitchen, her rending cries if she was hurt. When she was reading *The Lion, the Witch and the Wardrobe* she said I was like Mr Tumnus (something to do with my wiry hair). Telling me off about smoking even though I was doing it outside in the yard, in all weathers, wind and snow whirling about me.

*

Even though I'd lived here for a couple of years I couldn't get used to the place. Even though people would shout hello across the street, stop and chat about the Villa and whether Stan Collymore was any good, I didn't feel part of things here. I'd grown up just down the road but it could have been another city. Ironing one Saturday afternoon, listening to the football on the radio, I was looking out into the back garden, the bare laburnum framed in the window above the low square hedge. A leaf scraped along the path in a light wind, I could hear the cars and lorries moving always just beyond, out of sight. It seemed wrong. I couldn't get it to seem familiar to me.

She was ill, she had a pain in her chest. She called it her 'fear' pain. She was on the verge of being sick all the time. She wouldn't go to the doctor. I started to feel coming back from work like I did with Barbara in our last years together and wondered whether all relationships ended up heading this way; this one had got there much quicker. I stayed out longer on the pools round. Started attending matches. Stan Collymore wasn't any good.

Two years almost to the night she came out of the house all dressed up like that first time. I was just arriving home. Even from my distance I could see she wasn't an expert at applying make-up. She didn't seem to see me and walked off down the street. I followed her but she just walked down to the land underneath the motorway and wandered among the pillars holding up the rising road. I went back. She returned about an hour later, said nothing.

I wondered should I get help, call a doctor or something. Instead I called Bernie. The number I eventually found on the back of an envelope wasn't London, but a Coventry one. There was no reply but I left a message. Could she just come and see her mother, could she just come and talk to her? It would mean so much.

*

'Hello Dave,' I heard as I came in, dripping wet from the round.

I wouldn't have known it was her daughter, must have taken after the father, except for the pale skin which brought out roses in Bernie, as opposed to her mother's milder, more mottled colouring: age.

Kath was watching the television – Michael Barrymore's *Strike It Lucky* (early on she'd wanted us to apply to go on that show but I hadn't wanted to have the piss taken out of me) – and keeping her eye on her daughter. I dripped, took my coat off, ran my hands through my wet hair, went to the kitchen, and came back. I thought they must have had the big conversation, or Kath was so pleased to see her she could hardly speak, beyond the usual exclamations – 'Well, look at you!' Actually Bernie wasn't tall and didn't look glamorous to me. She wore trainers, dull green tracksuit bottoms, splashed with rain. She chewed gum, and looked around frowning at the room. When Kath went upstairs Bernie leaned forward and asked what tale Kath was spinning now.

It turned out she wasn't a drama student, though she had applied once. She was working in a hotel. Assistant Manager, she reckoned. I thought of Ruth, who I was seeing at the weekend (Imran's, Balsall Heath), as Bernie went on to detail her mother's crimes. She was lazy, selfish, nuts. Hadn't I noticed?

'You could try being sympathetic,' I said.

'Tried that,' she said, 'so did Dad, and look where it got him. Wrecked his life. Probably Frank's too – but who gives a toss about him?'

We heard the toilet flush, movement upstairs.

'Are you going to visit her again?' I hoped not, I was bristling, could have smacked her, but I was thinking of Kath.

'Nah,' she said, 'Don't see much point. And you? You going to stay the course?' She got up, stretched herself.

'Yes,' I said, feeling a last raindrop run down under my collar. 'I'm starting on the decorating next week.'

THE HEEBIE-JEEBIES

Barry took the tab at breakfast with his coffee. He skimmed through the mail – now he was fifty he could have £100 off his next car insurance and might win a trip around the world. He didn't drive. He had timed everything perfectly but the delivery – due at nine – was late. The drug was already kicking in and he was beginning to feel light and strange in his own room as the man with the large ears and little nose unpacked boxes and complained about yesterday's customers.

'Not a jot on the floor, naked kids running about and the latest widescreen and all the works.' Barry tried to keep up with the man's dark eyes, which shifted around too quickly in their sockets. 'Have you got sweets in?' Barry thought he heard and when he shrugged was told, 'For the kids tonight. Little beggars won't leave you alone.'

Barry said there was no need to set it up, he worked in an electrical shop and could manage but by then the man was on all fours laying cable and squatting to demonstrate the various sound options.

'Hall. Live. Rock. You name it. Orchestral.' He waved the remote like a baton. He talked as if he lived here and Barry was the visitor.

Wasn't it good now though to hear Hendrix as he'd never heard him, from five speakers? The lazy guitar of 'Hey Joe'. He lay back on the sofa and dropped through to other sofas and rooms he'd lain in and been at ease. Way back on the green settee with Nina, his girlfriend for two months, when her parents were out. Parties where everybody reclined on scatter cushions, conversation limited by the bass-heavy dub reggae and no dancing either, you had to be cool, only getting up to kneel over the huge bong when it came round. At weekends there was sometimes dancing, after acid or mescaline in pills or on blotting paper. He remembered tripping on the flare of his loons (which had to touch the floor) and making it into a dance move. Girls had whirled skirts and hair out in circles to Zep or Cream or Caravan; and later under stairs or in bathrooms he'd got handfuls of tit and tastes of them.

The regrouping in pubs and cafés the following weekend, pubs closed at 2 p.m., to discuss what happened after, how they got home in such a state, breathless and dodging skinheads. How they had outwitted drunken lungers, and negotiated dangerous roads where cars were out to eat you. How this one spent the night in the brand new toilets of the motorway service station – 'excellent facilities' – and that one was nearly fucked by a donkey when he slept in a barn; how all somehow had seen the sun rise from the side of a road or under a hedge, the fields and back lanes, the edge of town of his youth.

When Barry and Maxine moved in together, they tried to get more sophisticated: instead of getting out of their heads straight away they would have dinner parties with candles, meals of nut roast and sweet potatoes and play Dylan and Roxy Music until they finished the Vienetta and got out the big Rizlas and put on Peter Tosh or Burning Spear.

He remembered Maxine's fads, how she grew out of fringed leather jackets and boots quickly, moved on to the multicoloured waistcoats. When she only wore that. How she got into Italian food when the restaurant opened in town; the stray cats she fed out the back; her languor on Sundays lying the length of the sofa (like him now), bringing her chocolates and drinks and rewarded with sex.

He tried to read the free paper pushed through the door but the headlines merged: 'Queen Eats Ambassador's Son', 'Freed Man Topples Bridge', and little wavering flames swung up from between the lines of print to print him with burns.

He lay on turf with dripping water nearby and a hidden but throbbing power station, the leaning tower of Nina helped him with his tea.

The doorbell rang a second time and it was Tom. 'Howdy, pardner.' He was panting from the bike ride across town and pushed his vehicle in straight through to the kitchen.

'Didn't know if you'd be in,' he said.

'Coffee? Bong? Pills?'

*

'"I'm from the National Blonde Service," she said to me,' Tom said to him, leaning back on his chair and stretching out long legs. Barry could hear the faint pops and cracks of sinews and gristle and saw how they coloured the air around Tom. His friend's head went back when he exhaled as if pushed back by the smoke, an elephant's trunk of it, he still had hanks of hair hanging either side of his head, left from the days when it was abundant and flowing.

'People on top of the world,' said Tom, 'how do they keep their balance?' Then he stopped to lift and blow into an imaginary saxophone as 'Mirror in the Bathroom' broke out; nodding in praise of the new system.

They tried to make packet soup but ended up eating rubble with gulps of warm water. Luckily there was a lot of chocolate.

'You prepared well, captain,' said Tom, eyeing bars in the fridge, and turned to salute him.

'Danke shön, mein herr.' He didn't know why he'd turned German.

They bumped into each other on the stairs. They talked as if they'd met in the countryside, on the stairs there, as if wind was ruffling their hair and they had ruddy complexions.

Finally Barry bundled him out, bike and all, both vowing they would grow up soon, glancing up and down a street that seemed to come out of fog and concertina in and out around him, for the next interruption. The second phase of the drug was settling in, one that went right to his extremities, and he wanted to wank, wank longly over Maxine and Nina both. Maxina. Mixed up together for him and with only his pleasure in mind. But he'd only got to the first imaginings, Maxine with Nina's legs, when the doorbell rang again.

*

Maxine. She walked in as if out of a cubist painting, both eyes on the same side of her angular face, which was wrong because if Maxine was known for anything it was the roundness of her face. He couldn't be sure it was her who he'd been picturing so recently. A voice came from her that was the same, similar, but he couldn't place the tone or manner, even the accent.

'OK, OK,' he heard himself say to himself and turned away from her dark maroon-patterned clothes with yellow buttons like beams of light, torches into his room. First time he'd seen her she was in a yellow top, blouse with wide cuffs, some kind of matching hairband too, in the days when those things were worn.

He sat opposite her and momentarily his back slipped into place so that the pain he'd been experiencing, even through the drugs, seemed turned off. The room stopped tilting. Maxine's presence seemed to tighten the paintings above her, colours began to brim, the carpet seemed to breathe too, beneath its crust of dust, as if someone had finally cleaned it properly now she ran her eyes over it and around the crowded, smoky room. Each object she looked at sprang to attention.

'Good sound system.'

'Came today.'

She had long curtains of hair back then, everyone did, John Lennon-style. He could see her coming through a crowd. Her large pink mouth, slight Elvis curl to it, her little blue eyes, magnified by glasses, too little she said but he liked them, cheekiness there and something else besides, held back in them. Now her hair is a bob, shortish but still thick, the grey dyed out, curling at the ends. Her glasses almost invisible. Her mouth pursed, thinner of course, but not as thin as his – like lines drawn, he'd been told.

The *I'm fine thank yous* put out into the room, the settling down of each, the drawing of herself upright as if drawing a line for him to look at, slumped, unshaven and drugged across from her.

Of course after awkwardness they got deep into everyone they mutually knew and how they were doing and who had died – heart attack, lung cancer, overdose – starting with their immediate families and working outwards. When he talked back to her he kept tonguing the inside of his front teeth, the curve of the gum, that's where the taste was. They laughed about his mother, still singing Shirley Bassey songs off-key and scowling at the clatter of the letterbox, the ring of the doorbell. 'I do that,' he said, 'did it when you called, must be hereditary.' They went through friends, married and divorced, rich – relatively – and poor. Did she still see Stephen and Alice? She didn't.

She'd cut herself off, gone self-employed, when her new husband and then her lover left. Craft job, did some teaching at an FE college. Teaches the poor darlings to bury treasure, he thought he heard her say. He said he was doing the same as when she left which was almost true. Same job, slight promotion, different shop.

Next was books and films they'd watched and read and they snapped fingers over the same things like Alice Sebold and *Goodfellas*, even *Blade Runner* – 'Had you left by then?' he asked incredulously. Aaa-ceed! Chemical Brothers – they both put their hands in the air. She didn't get on with Britpop though, Oasis – turned her nose up.

To make her wrinkle it again he said he liked jazz but he only had one compilation, 'Music for Pleasure' at that, and he laughed at her reaction and confessed straight away that he didn't really, but got out Sufjan Stevens and Sparklehorse CDs to show he'd kept up. He played 'Chicago', but said he should play something from then, maybe the group Chicago (postcard of Chicago he'd had, Sears Tower in his head), something you could think of as their song, something off *After the Goldrush*, but he couldn't find it, and she said anyway their song had to be Slade, 'Cum on Feel the Noize', because that's the first song they'd danced to.

'At the YM disco?'

'At the YM disco.'

She accepted a joint from him, confessing it had been a while as their fingers touched, thumbs and indexes. She had come, she didn't tell him, to hear him play music again, smell and see him across a room, to put a box around a past that was coming up from pavements and found around corners, how pictures were forming of him and them all the time.

There was a smell of sweet oil in the room she must have brought with her. Perfume maybe. There were bright two-foot beings sat either side of her, bathing the room in light from their smiles. He could see the shape of her silhouetted in the light. Her shin the same, the one visible, and her knees, just showing below her dress. The calves too looked familiar, behind the shin and the knee never changing.

He put on 'Setting Sun' to 'change her mind about Noel Gallagher' and the room was full of the sweeping music. He had to blur his fingers and wave his arms and she laughed and got up to join him. They danced in slow motion/fast motion like the crazed cops on the video, falling into one another at the end.

When she sat down he put on Curved Air's 'Back Street Luv', which he'd found again recently and downloaded. 'Wow!' she said and when he put on Gregory Isaac's 'Loving Pauper' and the voice started up she said, 'You bastard.'

*

When he got up to shuffle to the kitchen he moved as if 'Rebel Rebel' was still playing even though the music had stopped, and she followed to the room where little sunlight penetrated but which seemed sun-filled now. It had leaked in from the angels who were dissolving away in the other room. She tapped his shoulder and touched his side, was to the front of him, to the side of him, helping him with cups and kettle and turning on taps, tutting at his fridge, moving with jar and spoon as if she'd often done that here. As if he'd opened his eyes in a place where things persisted.

They ate toast in there and recalled their cat – not the strays, the one that stayed with its fat stripy tail like a racoon's. At the door at night they'd call 'Here, child substitute, here subby, subby.' He remembered it wasn't long after its flattened death on the road that she left; some guy had been parked up around the corner for months, some guy she went to meet in the lounge bar of a near-empty pub on the newly-built ring road.

The taste of that time like soap and salt came back to him and he turned away, pretending to cough, particles of Marmite and crust spat into his hand. Then he started back and collapsed, shaking. The floor tiles where so many things had smashed cooled the length of him. He shuffled up, back against the wall and drew his knees up.

She leant towards him. 'You OK, Bas? Bas, speak to me.'

'It's OK, OK,' he said, his body had shuddered at her touch but now calmed. 'I'm OK. It's the drugs. I'll be there in a minute.'

*

When they got back in the front room and put down drinks and food, she sat on the sofa and asked if she could take off her shoes, which he helped her do and felt again the slopes of her feet and the knobs of her toes and the curl under them.

The light had faded, fog-rain at the window, the house swaddled in cloud. He felt for her leg then and she let him.

His fingertips were alive with this new Maxine, the same Maxine, the same stretch of moles and freckles along the inside of her thigh to the centre of her. She moved to let him try things, to move her back and undo and sit back to take her in, what was the same, what was different, nipples grown and spread the same pink as her lips, her skin generally darker though and the belly protruding, nicks and bumps acquired without him, marking her up, but under it the same Maxine that he put his fully-clothed arms around and felt contact with along the length of him, the same Maxine he clung to back in days more raw and fresh.

*

They moved upstairs. Why had he taken her to the box room that smelt of damp and had crumbled or coming-apart books on the window sill and ledge? Posters were stacked in cracked frames in a corner, ash- and dust-laden, the bed cold and resisting as they tried to get in but lay on top of instead, shivery and laughing while she leant to undress him finally.

Would she keep from laughing when she saw his uncut toenails, his patch of grey pubic hair? Maybe his beer belly would hide it, that new fixture he'd built on himself since she'd been gone. He hadn't flossed since 1992. Only now did he worry about the toilet she would use, the spider in the bath, the ring of dirt, the odour from the towel, the soap she would have to tug free of its recess.

He moved into her embrace, her breasts so much bigger now, burgeoning under his ribs. He'd forgotten just how small she was. He looked down at her eyes, clear as ever but with that depth, looking up at him through blackened lashes, the subtle pinkish eyeshadow on the creases of her lids when she blinked.

He remembered fucking her, how she joined in his conceits, pretending to be his secretary – very bourgeois, they'd laughed – or strangers meeting in a pub, maybe that planted the seed, the boots and lingerie she wore for him, but now was nothing like that, it was her wrapped around him strongly, pulling him deep as she could. It was a feeling out beyond the drugs but taking those with it, pushing him deep and flat-out, everything in him. Their bones bumped, their flesh stuck together; smells of him and her, seaweed and baked bread, sweet sweat, deodorant entered the sterile unadorned room and made it different. Every time he came into this room, he was thinking, as he felt her all over him, her grasp and thoughts and flesh around him, she would be there.

He didn't want to collapse on her, but felt like it after a climax like a flare gun going off in him ripped him up, and he managed to fall back away from her. Everything in him was suddenly mute, gone, and he woke up to find his ex-wife and recent lover slapping him gently. 'You blacked out,' she said, and for the second time: 'You OK?'

They lay back then side by side, eventually covering up their aged and pushed-out, mottled and dented bodies and flesh, half covering up: he could still see and touch her grown, flopping breasts. How the bulb light curved around her face, that cheek-and-nose shape, the tiny point of the nose like an apple pip in sight again.

'I remember when you got the heebie-jeebies,' she said, 'you wouldn't let anyone talk to you, not even me.' He nodded at this, but they didn't pursue any obvious trails of mutual memory, meeting, special signals, parting, not past one or two sentences about a place and a time.

She hadn't got what she'd come for, couldn't name it anyway, and now felt content to have him coming down beside her, his speech and movement slowing.

'Thought of you on your fiftieth,' she did tell him. 'Was out of the country but you know can't forget the date.'

They moved together again, him stroking her, and promising to cook a curry later, a skill he hadn't lost, when there were three rings on the bell downstairs. Maxine laughed when she realized it was trick-or-treaters and curled into him when he complained about Americanization, and lay like grace had descended in a warmth remembered and different. Outside the fog thickened as groups of skeletons and monsters and vampires laid siege to the street. Barry and Maxine got closer, balled up in each other, intertwining rough old flesh as kids outside started egging the house, spraying it with paint and flour, and letting off early fireworks, jumping jacks and bangers.

About the Author

© Simon Cooper

Born in Tewkesbury, Alan Beard, married with teen-age daughters, has lived in Birmingham for twenty-five years. He works as a librarian for Birmingham City University and is secretary of a successful writers' group. His stories have been broadcast on BBC Radio 4 and in many literary magazines and anthologies in England and the USA. His previous collection *Taking Doreen out of the Sky* (Picador) was widely praised.

Acknowledgements

With thanks to Tindal Street Press staff, particularly Alan Mahar and Luke Brown, and all in my writers' group past and present who have helped me and kept me going.

In memory of two friends and members of Tindal Street Fiction Group: Godfrey Featherstone (1939-2005) and Stuart Crees (1951-2005).

The following stories have been published elsewhere:

'Hot Little Danny' – published on pulp.net, 2005

'Backing Up' – runner up in the *The New Writer* 2007 Short Story Competition and published in *The New Writer* 2009

'Above the Shop' – published in *Pretext*, 2000

'The Party' – published in Parkes, N. & J. Bell (eds.), *Tell Tales 3* (Tell Tales Publishing, 2006)

'The Lookout' – published in *Frieze*, 1999, to accompany artwork by David Thorpe and in Bell, J. & J. Gay (eds.), *England Calling* (Weidenfeld & Nicholson, 2001)

'At the Back of Everything' – published first as 'Mustard' in *Sunk Island Review*, 2008, sunkislandreview.blogspot.com

'Background Noise' and 'The Heebie-Jeebies' – published on *East of the Web*, 2009, www.eastoftheweb.com

'Staff Development' – published in *The Warwick Review,* 2010

'The Ditch' – forthcoming in *Even More Tonto Stories* (Tonto Books, 2010)

'Huddersfield versus Crewe' – published in Royle, N. (ed.), *Neonlit* (Quartet Books, 1998), and in Beard, A. (ed.), *Going the Distance* (Tindal Street Press, 2003)